LOVE AND YOUTH

IVAN TURGENEV

LOVE AND YOUTH

Essential Stories

Translated from the Russian
by Nicolas Pasternak Slater and Maya Slater

PUSHKIN PRESS
LONDON

Pushkin Press
71–75 Shelton Street
London WC2H 9JQ

First Love was first published as *Pervaya lyubov* (**Первая любовь**)
in *Biblioteka Dlya Chteniya* (Saint Petersburg, March 1860)

'Bezhin Meadow' was first published as 'Bezhin lug'
(**Бежин луг**) in *A Sportsman's Sketches* (1852)

'Biryuk' was first published as 'Biryuk' (**Бирюк**)
in *A Sportsman's Sketches* (1852)

'The Rattling' was first published as 'Stuchit!'
(**Стучит!**) in *A Sportsman's Sketches* (1852)

'The District Doctor' was first published as 'Uyezdnyi lekar'
('**Уездный лекарь**') in *A Sportsman's Sketches* (1852)

'The Lovers' Meeting' was first published as as *Svidaniye*
('**Свидание**') in *A Sportsman's Sketches* (1852)

This translation first published by Pushkin Press in 2020

1 3 5 7 9 8 6 4 2

ISBN 13: 978-1-78227-601-2

Frontispiece: © Classic Image / Alamy Stock Photo

Typeset by Hewer Text UK Ltd, Edinburgh

Printed and bound in Great Britain by TJ Books Limited,
Padstow, Cornwall on Munken Premium White 80gsm

www.pushkinpress.com

CONTENTS

FIRST LOVE

THE OTHER GUESTS had left long ago. The clock struck half past midnight. The host, and Sergei Nikolaevich, and Vladimir Petrovich, were the only people left in the room.

The host rang for the remains of their dinner to be cleared away.

'So that's agreed,' he said, settling himself deeper in his armchair and lighting a cigar. 'Each of us has to tell the story of his first love. Sergei Nikolaevich, you start.'

Sergei Nikolaevich, a plump little man with a chubby, fair-skinned face, first looked at his host and then stared up at the ceiling.

'I never had a first love,' he said finally. 'I started with my second.'

'How did that happen?'

'Very simply. I was eighteen when I had my first flirtation, with a most attractive young lady. But I courted her as if I'd done it all before, just the way that later on I courted other girls. In point of fact, I fell in love for the first and last time when I was six, and it was with my nurse. But that was a very long time ago. I can't remember anything about our relationship—and even if I could, who'd be interested?'

'So what are we to do?' began the host. 'There was nothing particularly interesting about my first love either. I never fell in love with anyone till I met Anna Ivanovna, who's now my wife; and everything went perfectly smoothly for us, our parents arranged the match, we soon found we were in love, and got married as quickly as we could. My story can be told in a couple of words. I must admit, gentlemen, that when I raised the question of our first loves, I was relying on you—I won't say old bachelors, but bachelors who aren't as young as you were. Have you anything entertaining to tell us, Vladimir Petrovich?'

Vladimir Petrovich, a man of about forty with black hair just turning grey, hesitated a little and then said, 'My first love, it's true, was rather out of the ordinary.'

'Aha!' said the host and Sergei Nikolaevich in unison. 'All the better . . . Tell us about it.'

'Very well . . . Or no, I shan't tell it, I'm not good at storytelling. It either comes out too short and sketchy, or too wordy and affected. If you don't mind, I'll write down all I can remember in a notebook, and then read it to you.'

At first his friends wouldn't have this, but Vladimir Petrovich insisted. Two weeks later they met again, and he kept his promise.

Here is the story in his notebook:

I

It happened in the summer of 1833, when I was sixteen.

I was living in Moscow with my parents. They had rented a dacha for the summer near the Kaluga gate, opposite Neskuchny Gardens. I was studying for my university entrance, but I was taking it easy and doing very little work.

No one interfered with my freedom. I did what I liked, especially once I had parted from my tutor, a Frenchman who could never get over the fact that he had fallen into Russia 'like a bomb' (*'comme une bombe'*), and spent days lying on his bed with a sour look on his face. My father was affectionate but offhand with me. Mother took almost no notice of me, though she had no other children. She was fully occupied with other worries. My father, still a young and very handsome man, had made a marriage of convenience: she was ten years older than him. She lived a melancholy life, always anxious, jealous and crotchety, except in his presence. She was very frightened of him; he was stern, cold and distant with her . . . I have never known a calmer, more composed, confident and controlling man than him.

I shall never forget my first weeks in that dacha. The weather was beautiful; we moved there from town on the ninth of May, St Nicholas's day. I went for walks either in our own garden, or in Neskuchny Gardens, or outside the city gates, taking some book or other with me, perhaps Kaidanov's textbook; but I hardly ever opened it, and mostly just recited poetry aloud to myself—for I knew a lot of poetry by heart. My blood was in a ferment, my heart ached so sweetly and absurdly; I was endlessly waiting for something, dreading something, filled with wonder and anticipation; my imagination fluttered and soared and returned to the same fancies over and again, like martins circling a bell tower at sunrise; I was dreamy, and gloomy, and even wept; but through my very sorrows and tears, brought on perhaps by the music of a verse or a beautiful evening, there sprang up, like the fresh grass in springtime, a joyful sense of youth and burgeoning life.

I had a horse to ride, and I used to saddle it myself and wander far away on my own, breaking into a gallop and imagining that I was a jousting knight . . . How merrily the wind whistled in my ears! . . . Or I would just turn my face up to the sky, to fill my thirsty soul with its radiant azure light.

At the time, I remember, the image of a woman, the idea of love, hardly ever took definite shape in my mind; yet behind everything I thought and felt, there lay hidden a half-aware, shy presentiment of something new, something unutterably sweet and feminine . . .

That presentiment, that expectation, flooded my whole being. I breathed it, it flowed through my veins in every drop of my blood . . . And it was soon to come true.

Our dacha consisted of the main wooden house, with a colonnade, and two small lodges. The lodge on the left housed a tiny workshop making cheap wallpapers. I had gone in there several times to watch a dozen skinny, scruffy youths with drink-sodden faces, wearing greasy smocks. They kept jumping in the air to grab the wooden levers and press down the rectangular wooden blocks of the press, using the weight of their puny bodies to print out the brightly coloured wallpaper designs. The lodge on the right stood empty and was rented out. One day, some three weeks after the ninth of May, the shutters of that building were opened up and I saw women's faces at the windows. A family had moved in. At lunch that same day, I remember my mother asking our servant who our new neighbours were. When she heard the name of Princess Zasekina, she first commented respectfully, 'Ah! A princess . . .' but then added, 'She must be quite hard up.'

'Arrived in three hired cabs, madame,' replied the servant, deferentially offering her a dish. 'They don't have a carriage of their own, and their furniture's very ordinary.'

'Yes,' returned my mother. 'But it's better that way.'

My father cast her a frigid glance, and she fell silent.

And indeed, Princess Zasekina could not have been a rich woman. The little house she had rented was so ancient, and small, and squat, that no one even moderately well off could have chosen to live there. But at the time, all this went in one ear and out of the other. I was not particularly impressed by her princely title—I had just read Schiller's *The Robbers*.

II

Every evening I used to stroll round our garden with my shotgun, on the lookout for rooks. I had long detested these wary, crafty and rapacious birds. On that particular day I went out into the garden, and after I had been down all the paths without seeing any rooks (they had recognized me, and were just cawing sporadically in the distance), I happened to approach the low fence that separated our own grounds from the narrow strip of the right-hand lodge garden. I was walking with my head bowed. Suddenly I heard voices, and when I looked over the fence, I was thunderstruck by the strange sight that met my eyes.

A few paces away, on the grass among the leafy raspberry bushes, stood a tall, slender girl in a pink striped dress with a white scarf tied round her head. Four young men crowded round her, and she was tapping each of them in turn on the brow with a bunch of those small grey flowers—I don't remember their name, but children know them very well. The flowers grow little pods which burst with a snap if you strike them against something hard. The young men were offering their foreheads so eagerly, and the girl's movements (I was looking at her from the side) were so enchanting, imperious, caressing, mocking and sweet, that I almost cried out in astonishment and delight. I think I would have given anything in the world just to have those lovely little fingers tap me on my forehead too. My gun slipped onto the grass. I forgot everything, while my eyes devoured her graceful form, her neck, her beautiful arms, her slightly ruffled fair hair under its white scarf, and her alert, narrowed eye, and those eyelashes, and the soft cheek beneath them . . .

'Young man! Hey, you, young man!' said a voice beside me suddenly. 'Do you think you ought to be staring at young ladies you don't know?'

I started, and froze where I stood. On the far side of the fence, a man with short black hair was standing quite close to me and giving me an ironic look. And at that very moment, the girl turned towards me. I saw a pair of large grey eyes in a lively, excited face, and suddenly she was quivering with laughter all over that face of hers, her white teeth were glistening, her eyebrows seemed to be raised . . . Red in the face, I grabbed my gun from the grass and fled, pursued by ringing laughter that had no malice to it. I ran off to my room, flung myself down on my bed and covered my face with my hands. My heart was pounding. I was bitterly ashamed, and yet glad; I had never felt so excited in my life.

When I recovered, I brushed my hair, cleaned myself up and went down to tea. The image of that young girl hovered before me; my heart had stopped pounding, but was filled with a kind of delicious tension.

'What's wrong?' asked my father suddenly. 'Shot a rook?'

I wanted to tell him all about it, but I held my tongue and just smiled to myself. I don't know why, but when I retired to my room, I spun round three times on one leg, pomaded my hair, got into bed and slept like a dead man all night. In the early morning I woke for a moment, raised my head, looked around in delight, and went back to sleep.

III

'How can I get to know them?' That was my first thought when I woke next morning. I went out into the garden before my morning tea, but without going too close to the fence; and I saw no one. After my tea I walked up and down the road in front of the dacha a few times and looked into the windows from a distance . . . I thought I saw her face behind a curtain, took fright and hurried away. 'I really have to meet her,' I thought, pacing distractedly up and down the sandy patch of ground outside Neskuchny Park. 'But how? That is the question.' I recalled every detail of our meeting the day before: for some reason I remembered particularly clearly how she had laughed at me. But even as I made one anxious plan after another, fate had already lent a helping hand.

While I was out, a letter had come for my mother from our new neighbour. It was written on grey paper and sealed with brown sealing wax, the kind that is only used on notes from the post office or the corks of cheap wine bottles. In this half-illiterate, messily written letter, the princess begged my mother to use her influence to help her: in the princess's words, my mother was closely acquainted with highly placed persons who could decide the fate of herself and her children, since she was involved in very important lawsuits. 'Im writing you,' she went on, 'as one Gentlewoman to another, and its a Great plesure for me too take this opertunity too do so.' In conclusion, she begged my mother's permission to pay her a visit. I found my mother very much put out. My father was not at home, and she had nobody to ask for advice. Not to answer this 'Gentlewoman'—and a princess at that—was unthinkable. But how to answer her? She had no idea. It seemed wrong to send her a note in French, but my mother's own Russian spelling was uncertain. She was aware of it, and didn't want to expose herself. She was relieved when I came in, and at once told me to step round to the princess and tell her that my mother would always be happy to serve Her Excellency in any way she could, and to invite her over after midday. I was half delighted and half scared to have my secret desires fulfilled so promptly and unexpectedly, but I hid my confusion and ran upstairs to my room to put on a new tie and tailcoat. At home I was still going round in short jackets and soft collars, which I hated.

IV

I couldn't help trembling all over as I stepped into the cramped, untidy hallway of the lodge. I was met by a grey-haired old servant with a swarthy, copper-coloured face, surly little piggy eyes, and the deepest furrows on his forehead and temples that I had ever seen. On the dish he was carrying lay a herring-bone, gnawed clean. Holding the door to the next room open with his foot, he snapped: 'What do you want?'

'Is Princess Zasekina home?' I asked.

'Boniface!' cried a quavering female voice from inside the room.

Without a word, the servant turned his back on me, displaying the threadbare back of his livery coat with its single rusty crested button. He put the plate down on the floor and went away.

'Have you been to the police?' called the same female voice. The servant muttered something in reply. 'Eh? Someone's called?' the voice repeated. 'The young gentleman from next door? Well, ask him in, then.'

'Will you step into the drawing room?' said the servant, reappearing in front of me and picking up the plate.

I straightened my clothes and went into what they called the 'drawing room'.

I found myself in a small, rather untidy room with cheap furniture that seemed to have been hastily arranged around it. By the window, in an easy chair with a broken arm, sat a woman of about fifty, bareheaded and ugly, in an old green dress; she had a woollen scarf with a garish pattern round her neck. Her small dark eyes bored into my face.

I went up to her and bowed.

'Do I have the honour of speaking to Princess Zasekina?'

'Yes, I'm Princess Zasekina. Are you Mr V.'s son?'

'Yes, madame. My mother has sent me round with a message.'

'Do sit down. Boniface! Where are my keys? Have you seen them anywhere?'

I passed on my mother's reply to the princess's note. She heard me out, tapping on the windowsill with her podgy red fingers, and when I finished she fixed her eyes on me once more.

'Very well, I'll certainly come over,' she said at last. 'How young you seem! How old are you, might I ask?'

'Sixteen,' I answered hesitantly. The princess pulled some greasy scribbled sheets of paper from her pocket, brought them right up to her nose and began to leaf through them.

'That's a good age,' she suddenly announced, turning round and shuffling her chair. 'Now please, don't stand on ceremony with me. We're free and easy here.'

'Too free and easy,' I thought, eyeing her unattractive person with involuntary distaste.

At that moment another door was thrown open and a girl appeared, the one I had seen in the garden the day before. She raised a hand, and gave me a mocking smile.

'And here's my daughter,' said the princess, gesturing at her with an elbow. 'Zinochka, this is our neighbour Mr V.'s son. What's your name, may I ask?'

'Vladimir,' I whispered, rising to my feet in confusion.

'And after your father? . . .'

'Petrovich.'

'Ah! I used to know a police inspector called Vladimir Petrovich, like you. Boniface! No need to hunt for the keys, they're in my pocket.'

The girl was still looking at me with that mocking smile, narrowing her eyes and cocking her head a little to one side.

'I've already met Monsieur Voldemar,' she said. The sound of her silvery voice gave me a delicious shiver. 'Will you allow me to call you that?'

'By all means,' I stammered.

'Where was that?' asked the princess; but her daughter did not reply.

'Are you busy just now?' she asked me, not taking her eyes off me.

'Not at all.'

'Would you like to help me wind some wool? Come along to my room.'

She nodded to me and left the room; I followed her.

The furniture in her room was of rather better quality, and arranged with more taste. Though at that moment I noticed almost nothing—I was moving as if in a dream, my whole being filled with a stupid sort of intense bliss.

The young princess sat down, took up a skein of red wool and motioned me to sit on the chair opposite her. Then she carefully loosened the skein and draped it over my hands. All this she did in silence, with a sort of comical deliberation, and still with that same bright, sly smile on her half-open lips. She started winding the wool onto a folded piece of card, and suddenly directed such a quick and dazzling glance at me that I could not help lowering my eyes. When she fully opened her own eyes, which she generally kept half-closed, her face was quite transformed, as though flooded with light.

'What did you think of me yesterday, Monsieur Voldemar?' she asked after a pause. 'You probably judged me harshly?'

'I . . . Princess . . . I didn't think anything . . . how could I . . .' I answered in confusion.

'Listen,' she took me up. 'You don't know me yet. I'm a very strange person. I want people always to tell me the truth. I'm told you're sixteen. I'm twenty-one; so you see I'm much older than you, and that means you always have to tell me the truth . . . and do what I tell you,' she added. 'Look at me. Why don't you look at me?'

I became even more embarrassed—but I looked up at her. She smiled, not with the same smile as before, but a different one, a smile of approval.

'Look at me,' she said again, lowering her voice affectionately. 'I don't mind . . . I like your face; I have a feeling we're going to be friends. Do you like me?' she added slyly.

'Princess . . .' I began.

'First of all, you must call me Zinaida Alexandrovna. And secondly, what's the sense in children—' (she corrected herself) '—young people, I mean, not saying straight out what they feel? That's all very well for grown-ups. You do like me, don't you?'

Although I was greatly enjoying the way she talked so frankly to me, I was rather hurt. I wanted to prove that I wasn't a little boy, so I did my best to put on a nonchalant, serious air and announced:

'Of course, Zinaida Alexandrovna, I like you a lot. I wouldn't want to hide that.'

She very deliberately shook her head.

'Have you got a tutor?' she asked suddenly.

'No, I haven't had one for ages.'

I was lying. Not a month had passed since my Frenchman had left us.

'Oh! Yes, I see, you're quite grown up.'

She tapped me lightly on the fingers.

'Hold your arms out straight!'—And she carried on carefully winding her ball of wool.

She kept her eyes lowered, and I took advantage to begin watching her, first stealthily and then more and more boldly. Her face looked even more beautiful than the day before—everything about it was so delicate, intelligent and charming. She was sitting with her back to a window with a white blind over it. A sunbeam shining through the blind shed a soft light on her fluffy golden hair, her innocent neck, her sloping shoulders and tender, untroubled bosom. I gazed at her—how close and dear she was to me! I felt that I had known her for a very long time, and that before her, I had never known anything, nor ever lived . . . She was wearing a shabby, dark dress and an apron; I think I would have been happy to caress every fold of both dress and apron. The tips of her boots peeped out from under the hem of her dress: I could have knelt down in adoration before them. 'And here I am, sitting in front of her,' I thought, 'I've come to know her . . . my God, what happiness!' In my delight, I almost jumped up from my chair, but instead I just swung my legs a bit, like a child munching on a treat.

I felt as happy as a fish in water; I should have liked never to leave that room, nor move from my place.

Slowly she raised her eyelids, and once again her clear eyes shone gently at me—and once again she smiled.

'How you're looking at me!' she said slowly, wagging a forefinger at me.

I blushed. 'She understands everything—she sees everything!'—the thought flashed through my mind. 'And how could she fail to see and understand everything?'

Suddenly there were noises in the next room, and the clink of a sabre.

'Zina!' the old princess called from the drawing room. 'Belovzorov has brought you a kitten.'

'A kitten!' squealed Zinaida, leaping up from her chair. She tossed the ball of wool onto my knees and rushed out of the room.

I got up too, laid the skein and the ball of wool on the windowsill, and went back to the drawing room. There I halted in amazement. In the middle of the room lay a tabby kitten, its paws spread-eagled on the floor. Zinaida was on her knees beside it, gently raising its head. Standing by the old princess, and occupying almost the whole stretch of wall between the two windows, was a curly-headed blond young hussar with a ruddy complexion and bulging eyes.

'Isn't it funny!' Zinaida kept repeating. 'And its eyes aren't grey but green. And what big ears! Thank you, Viktor Yegorich. That was very sweet of you.'

The hussar, whom I recognized as one of the young men I had seen the day before, smiled and bowed, clicking his spurs and jingling his sabre chain.

'Yesterday you were good enough to say that you wished to have a tabby kitten with big ears . . . so I got one for you. Your word is law.' And he bowed once more.

The kitten gave a feeble mew and began sniffing the floor.

'It's hungry!' cried Zinaida. 'Boniface! Sonia! Bring some milk!'

A maid in an old yellow dress with a faded kerchief round her neck brought in a saucer of milk and placed it in front of the kitten. The kitten gave a start, blinked and began lapping it up.

'How pink its little tongue is,' remarked Zinaida, bending her head almost down to the floor and peering right under the kitten's nose.

After drinking its fill, the kitten purred and daintily licked its paws. Zinaida stood up, turned to the maid and said carelessly, 'Take it away.'

'In return for the kitten, I claim your hand,' simpered the hussar, drawing up his mighty frame tightly squeezed into a brand-new uniform.

'Both of them,' rejoined Zinaida, holding out her hands to him. As he kissed them, she looked over his shoulder at me.

I stood stock still, not knowing whether to laugh, say something or keep quiet. Suddenly, through the open doorway to the passage, I caught sight of our footman Fyodor making signs to me. I went out to him in a daze.

'What is it?' I asked.

'Your mama has sent for you,' he whispered. 'She is annoyed with you for not coming back with an answer.'

'Why, have I been here long?'

'Over an hour.'

'Over an hour!' I blurted out, returning to the drawing room and beginning to scrape my heels and make my bows.

'Where are you off to?' asked the young princess, looking at me over the hussar's shoulder.

'I have to go home. So I'll tell my mother,' I added to the old princess, 'that you'll pay us a visit after one o'clock.'

'Yes, young man, please do.'

Hurriedly she pulled out her snuffbox, and gave such a loud sniff that I started.

'Please do tell her,' she repeated with a grunt, blinking her rheumy eyes.

I bowed once more, turned and left the room, with that awkward tingle in my spine which any very young man has when he knows that everyone is watching him leave.

'Now mind, Monsieur Voldemar, mind you come back and see us,' cried Zinaida, bursting out laughing again.

'Why does she keep laughing?' I wondered as I walked home, while Fyodor followed silently behind me exuding disapproval. Mama scolded me and demanded to know what on earth had kept me so long at the princess's. I went straight up to my room without answering. I was suddenly feeling very sad, and trying hard not to cry . . . I was jealous of the hussar.

V

The princess called on my mother as she had promised. My mother did not take to her. I wasn't present at their meeting, but at dinner Mama told my father that she found this Princess Zasekina *une femme très vulgaire*. The princess had annoyed my mother by repeatedly begging her to intercede with Prince Sergey on her behalf; she seemed to be engaged in endless lawsuits— *des vilaines affaires d'argent*—and must be a terrible troublemaker. But then my mother added that she had invited the princess and her daughter to dinner next day (on hearing the word 'daughter', I buried my nose in my plate), because when all was said and done, she was our neighbour and a titled lady. To this my father observed that he now remembered who this lady was. As a young man he had known the late Prince Zasekin, a very well-bred but absurdly empty-headed person, who had spent so long in Paris that he was nicknamed 'Le Parisien'. He used to be very rich, but lost his whole fortune at cards; and then for some reason, nobody knew why, though it might have been for money (and he could have made a better choice, added my father with a frosty smile), he had married the daughter of some business agent. After which he started speculating and hopelessly ruined himself.

'I hope she doesn't come asking for a loan,' remarked my mother.

'She may well do,' said my father calmly. 'Does she speak French?'

'Very badly.'

'Hmm. Anyway, that doesn't matter. I believe you said you'd invited her daughter too. Someone was telling me that she's a very pretty and cultured girl.'

'Ah! Then she doesn't take after her mother.'

'Nor her father either,' he replied. 'That man was quite well educated, but stupid.'

My mother sighed and looked thoughtful. My father said no more. I had been feeling very uncomfortable all through this conversation.

After dinner I went out into the garden, but without my gun. I had promised myself not to go near the Zasekins' garden, but an irresistible force drew me towards it, and with good reason. Even before I reached the fence, I caught sight of Zinaida. This time she was alone. She was holding a little book and walking slowly along the path. She did not notice me.

I very nearly let her pass by, but all at once I thought better of it and coughed.

She turned, but did not stop. Drawing back the broad blue ribbon of her round straw hat with her hand, she looked at me, smiled a gentle smile and fixed her eyes on her book again.

I took off my cap, hesitated a moment or two, and then walked away with a heavy heart. '*Que suis-je pour elle?*' I asked myself—in French, heaven knows why.

I heard familiar footsteps behind me. Looking round, I saw my father coming after me with his light, rapid step.

'Is that the young princess?' he asked.

'Yes.'

'Do you know her, then?'

'I met her this morning at her mother's.'

My father stopped, turned abruptly on his heels and went back. When he came up alongside Zinaida he bowed politely. She returned his bow, looking rather surprised, and lowered her book. I saw her following him with her eyes. My father was always very elegantly dressed, with a simple style of his own; but I had never seen him look so graceful, nor ever seen his grey hat sit so finely on his barely thinning hair.

I made to move towards Zinaida, but she did not even spare me a look. Raising her book again, she walked off.

VI

I spent all that evening and next morning in a state of numb misery. I tried to work, I remember, and picked up my Kaidanov; I stared and stared at the large print in that famous textbook, but it was no use. Ten times over I read the words 'Julius Caesar was renowned for his military prowess' but nothing got through to me, and I gave up. Before dinner I pomaded my hair and put on my tailcoat and tie again.

'What's all this for?' asked my mother. 'You aren't a student yet—heaven knows whether you'll pass your exams. And you haven't had your jacket long. You can't just throw it away!'

'We've got guests coming,' I whispered hopelessly.

'Rubbish! Guests indeed!'

I had to give in. I took off the tailcoat and put on my jacket instead, but I kept the tie on. The old princess and her daughter turned up half an hour before dinnertime. The mother was wearing a yellow shawl over the green dress I had already seen, and an old-fashioned cap with flame-coloured ribbons. She started straight off talking about her bills of exchange, sighing and complaining about how poor she was, whimpering about how she needed help, noisily sniffing her snuff, wriggling and twisting about on her chair, and utterly forgetting her dignity as a princess. Zinaida, for her part, held herself quite primly, almost haughtily, like a real princess. Her expression was so unbendingly cold and dignified that I barely recognized her; I had never seen her look like that or smile like that—but I found her just as beautiful like this. Her gauzy summer dress had a pale-blue motif on it. She wore her long hair down, framing her face in the English style, which matched the cold expression on her face. My father sat next to her during our meal, entertaining his neighbour with his characteristic calm, elegant courtesy. From time to time he would cast a glance at her—and she would glance at him, with a very strange, almost hostile look. They talked French, and I remember being astonished at the purity of her accent. During the meal, the old princess went on behaving with great freedom, eating a great deal and praising the food she was served. My mother was visibly bored with her, answering her questions with a kind of wan indifference. Occasionally my father gave a faint frown. My mother did not like Zinaida either.

'A stuck-up little miss,' she said next day. 'And what's she got to be so conceited about, *avec sa mine de grisette.*'

'You've obviously never seen any grisettes,' my father remarked.

'And thank goodness for that!'

'Well, thank goodness indeed—but how can you be judging them, then?'

Zinaida had not paid me the slightest attention during dinner, and as soon as it was over her mother began taking her leave.

'I shall hope for your kind offices, Marya Nikolaevna and Piotr Vasilyich,' she intoned to my mother and father. 'What can I do? We had some good times, but they're over now. And here I am—an excellency,' she went on with an unpleasant laugh, 'what a useless honour when we've nothing to eat!'

My father gave her a respectful bow and saw her to the hall door. I was standing right there, in my short little jacket, staring at the floor like a man condemned to death. I was utterly crushed by Zinaida's treatment of me. Imagine my amazement when, as she passed me, she quickly whispered, with the old affectionate look in her eyes, 'Come over at eight o'clock, do you hear? Without fail . . .'

I flung out my arms in surprise—but she was gone, throwing a white scarf over her hair as she went out.

VII

On the stroke of eight I walked into the hallway of the little lodge where the princess lived, wearing my tailcoat and with my hair brushed up in a quiff over my brow. The old servant gave me a morose look and got up unwillingly from his bench. I could hear merry voices coming from the drawing room. I opened the door, and stepped back in astonishment. The young princess was standing on a chair in the middle of the room, holding a man's hat in front of her, with five men gathered around the chair. Each was trying to dip a hand into the hat, which she was holding high in the air and shaking vigorously. When she caught sight of me, she cried out:

'Stop, wait! Here's another guest, he has to have a
ticket too!' Then she jumped down from the chair and
took me by my sleeve. 'Come on, then!' she said. 'What
are you waiting for? Messieurs, allow me to introduce
you: this is Monsieur Voldemar, our neighbours' son.
And these,' she added, turning to me and pointing out
her guests in turn, 'are Count Malevsky, Doctor
Lushin, Maidanov the poet, retired Captain Nirmatsky,
and Belovzorov, the hussar you've already met. I hope
you'll be friends.'

I was so embarrassed, I did not even bow to
anyone. I recognized Doctor Lushin as the same
dark-skinned gentleman who had so mercilessly
humiliated me in the garden. The others I had
never seen before.

'Count!' Zinaida went on, 'write out a ticket for
Monsieur Voldemar.'

'That's not fair,' objected the count, talking with a
slight Polish accent. He was a very handsome man,
stylishly dressed, with brown hair and expressive dark-
brown eyes, a narrow little white nose and a thin
moustache over his tiny mouth. 'This gentleman hasn't
been playing forfeits with us.'

'Yes, unfair,' echoed Belovzorov and the gentleman
described as a retired captain—a man of about forty,
repulsively pockmarked, frizzy-haired as a blackamoor,

round-shouldered, bow-legged, and dressed in an unbuttoned military tunic with no epaulettes.

'Go on, write him a ticket, I say,' repeated the princess. 'What's this, a mutiny? Monsieur Voldemar is here for the first time, and he's excused all the rules. There's no use grumbling, write it out, that's what I want.'

The count shrugged, bowed his head obediently, picked up a pen in his white hand with its many rings, tore off a scrap of paper and began writing.

'At least let us tell Monsieur Voldemar what's going on,' began Lushin sarcastically, 'otherwise he'll be completely in the dark. You see, young man, we're playing at forfeits; the princess has lost, and now whoever draws the lucky ticket will have the right to kiss her hand. Do you understand what I'm saying?'

I merely looked at him and remained standing there in bewilderment, while the princess jumped back onto the chair and began shaking the hat again. Everyone stretched their arms up, and I did the same.

'Maidanov,' said the princess to a tall young man with a thin face, half-blind little eyes and extremely long black hair, 'as a poet, you ought to be magnanimous and let Monsieur Voldemar have your ticket, so that he has two chances instead of just one.'

But Maidanov shook his head and tossed his hair aside. I took my turn last, dipped my hand into the hat, picked out a paper and unfolded it. Oh Lord! Imagine my feelings when I read the word 'Kiss!'

'A kiss!' I could not help crying out.

'Bravo! He's won,' said the princess. 'I'm so glad!' She stepped down off the chair and looked me in the eyes with such a bright, sweet gaze that my heart leapt up. 'Are you glad too?' she asked.

'Me? . . .' I stammered

'Sell me your ticket,' Belovzorov suddenly barked beside my ear. 'I'll give you a hundred roubles for it.'

I replied with a look of such indignation that Zinaida clapped her hands, while Lushin cried 'Well done!'

'But,' he went on, 'as master of ceremonies, I have to see that all the rules are observed. Monsieur Voldemar, get down on one knee. That's how we do things here.'

Zinaida stood in front of me, leaned her head a little to one side, as if to take a better look at me, and ceremoniously extended her hand. My head swam; I tried to get down on one knee, but sank onto both, and pressed my lips against Zinaida's fingers so clumsily that her fingernail gave my nose a slight scratch.

'Very good!' cried Lushin, and helped me to my feet.

The game of forfeits continued. Zinaida placed me next to her. What amazing penalties she thought up! She herself, for instance, had to pretend to 'be a statue'—and for her pedestal she chose ugly Nirmatsky, ordering him to lie face down on the floor and even bend his head down on his chest. The laughter never ceased for a second. I myself had had a dull, lonely upbringing in a traditional genteel home, and all this noise and uproar, this unconstrained and almost riotous merriment, these outrageous goings-on with complete strangers, utterly turned my head. I was as drunk as though from too much wine. I began laughing and chattering louder than anyone else, so that even the old princess, sitting in the next room with some clerk from the Iberian Gate whom she had summoned for a consultation, came out to take a look at me. But I was feeling so happy, I couldn't have cared less about people laughing at me or giving me odd looks.

Zinaida carried on making me her favourite, and kept me by her side. For one of my forfeits I found myself sitting next to her with both our heads under one silk scarf, and I was supposed to tell her *my secret*. I remember how both our heads suddenly found themselves in that steamy, half-transparent, fragrant darkness, with her eyes gently shining close to my face, her open lips breathing warm air onto me, and I saw her teeth, and the ends of her hair tickled my skin and set it on fire. I said nothing. She smiled a sly, mysterious smile, and eventually whispered 'Well then?', but I merely blushed and giggled, and turned my head away, barely able to breathe. Then we got tired of forfeits, and began playing the string game. My God! imagine my delight, when for a moment's absent-mindedness on my part, she gave me a hard, sharp smack on my fingers. After that, I did my best to pretend to have my head in the clouds, but she just teased me and never touched my outstretched hands again!

What didn't we get up to that evening! We played the piano, and sang, and danced, and pretended to set up a gypsy camp. We dressed Nirmatsky up as a bear, and made him drink salt water. Count Malevsky performed some card tricks, finally shuffling the pack for whist and dealing himself all the trumps, for which Lushin 'had the honour to congratulate him'. Maidanov declaimed some passages from his epic poem 'The Assassin' (this was the heyday of Romanticism); he planned to publish it in a black binding with the title in blood-coloured letters. The clerk from the Iberian Gate had his cap stolen off his knees, and in order to get it back he was made to perform a Cossack dance.

Old Boniface was decked out in a lady's cap, while the young princess put on a man's hat ... I couldn't go through all the things we did. Belovzorov alone retired further and further into a corner, scowling furiously. Sometimes his eyes would grow bloodshot, he would turn red in the face and seem to be about to hurl himself at us and scatter us in all directions like wood shavings. But when the princess looked at him and wagged a warning finger, he would retreat back into his corner.

At last we were exhausted. Even the old princess, though she was up for anything, as she put it, and didn't mind any amount of screaming, eventually felt tired and wanted to rest. Dinner was served shortly before midnight—a lump of stale dry cheese and some cold chopped ham pies, which I found more delicious than the most delicate pastries; there was only one bottle of wine, and that a rather peculiar one of dark-coloured glass with a wide neck, containing pink wine—anyway, no one drank any. Completely happy and quite exhausted, I left the lodge; as we parted, Zinaida squeezed my hand tightly and gave me another mysterious smile.

The night air was heavy and damp on my overheated face. There seemed to be a thunderstorm on the way, with black rain clouds advancing across the sky, growing larger and constantly changing their smoky shapes. The wind was gusting fitfully in the dark trees, and somewhere far away over the horizon, the muffled thunder was grumbling crossly to itself.

I came in through the back door and slipped upstairs to my room. The old servant who looked after me was asleep on the floor, so I had to step over him. He woke and saw me, and said that my mama was annoyed with me again and had wanted to send for me, but my father had stopped her. (I used never to go to bed without saying goodnight to her and asking for her blessing.) But there was nothing to be done.

I told the servant that I'd get undressed and put myself to bed on my own; and I blew out my candle. But I didn't get undressed, and I didn't go to bed.

I sat down on my chair and stayed sitting there like a man bewitched. What I was feeling was so new, and so delicious . . . I sat quite still, barely glancing this way and that, and breathing slowly. Now and then I laughed silently to myself, going over what had happened; or froze inwardly at the thought that I was in love, that this was it, this was love. Zinaida's countenance floated gently before my eyes in the darkness— floated in the air, without drifting away; her lips still smiled that enigmatic smile, her eyes gazed at me from one side, questioningly, thoughtfully and tenderly . . .

just as they had at the moment when we parted. At last I stood up and tiptoed to my bed; without undressing, I carefully lowered my head onto my pillow, as if afraid that any abrupt movement might disturb the sensations that flooded my being.

I lay down on the bed but never shut my eyes. Soon I noticed a succession of faint flashes of light shining into my room. I raised my head and looked out of the window. The window frame stood out sharply against the pale, mysterious light on the panes. 'A thunderstorm,' I thought to myself. And so it was, but very far away, too far to hear the thunder, though there was a constant flickering of faint, long, forked lightnings, not exactly flashing, but rather quivering and twitching like the wings of a dying bird. I got up, walked over to the window and stayed standing there till morning. The lightning flashes never ceased for an instant; it was what the peasants call a 'sparrows' night'. I looked out at the silent sandy expanse, at the dark shape of Neskuchny Gardens, the yellow façades of distant buildings, which also seemed to be twitching at each faint lightning flash . . . I gazed out, and couldn't tear myself away from the sight. Those silent lightnings, that shy flickering, seemed to echo the secret, wordless yearnings burning in my soul. The morning dawned; patches of crimson light announced daybreak. As the sun began to appear, the lightnings became fainter and more fleeting, quivering more and more rarely, and eventually vanishing altogether, drowned in the uncompromising, sober light of a new day.

And the lightnings within me vanished too. I felt a profound weariness and peace . . . but the image of Zinaida still hovered triumphantly over my soul. And yet this very image, too, seemed more tranquil: like a swan taking flight out of the reeds of a swamp, it separated itself from the unsightly images that surrounded it. As I fell asleep, I flung myself down before it for the last time, to bid it a trusting, adoring farewell.

Oh, you meek emotions, you gentle sounds, the goodness and peace of a softened heart, the melting joy of the first raptures of love—where are you now, where are you?

VIII

When I came down to tea next morning, my mother scolded me—but less than I had expected. She made me tell her what I had been doing the evening before. I answered her shortly, leaving out many of the details and trying to make the whole evening sound quite innocent.

'Even so, they're not *comme il faut*,' remarked my mother. 'And you've no business to be hanging about there instead of studying for your exams.'

I knew that my mother's concerns about my studies weren't going to go beyond those few words, so I didn't bother to argue with her. But after tea my father took my arm, walked me out into the garden and made me tell him everything that I had seen at the Zasekins'.

He had a strange influence over me—and our relations were strange ones too. He took almost no interest in my education, but he was never rude to me; he respected my freedom, and even treated me courteously, if one could call it that. But he never allowed me to get close to him. I loved him and admired him, he was my ideal of a man—and my God, how passionately I would have adored him, if I hadn't always felt him holding me at a distance! And yet he could awaken my boundless trust with a single word, a single gesture, in an instant, whenever he pleased. My soul would open up to him, and I would chat with him as though he were a wise friend or an indulgent teacher . . . And then, just as abruptly, he would drop me, and his hand would push me away—softly and gently, but it would push me away.

Sometimes he would indulge in a fit of high spirits, and then he would be happy to romp and play with me like a boy (he loved any kind of physical activity). Once—and only once!—he caressed me so tenderly that I almost burst into tears . . . But his high spirits, and his tenderness, would vanish without a trace; and whatever passed between us gave me no hopes for the future—I might as well have dreamt it all. I sometimes found myself gazing at his bright, handsome, intelligent face . . . my heart would tremble, my whole being would long to be close to him . . . and he would seem to sense what I was feeling, give me a casual pat on the cheek, and either go away, or take up some activity, or suddenly grow cold, the way he alone knew how to do—and I would instantly shrink into myself and turn cold too. His rare moments of friendliness were never in response to my eloquent though unspoken entreaties—they always came unexpectedly. When I later reflected on my father's character, I concluded that he wasn't really interested in me, nor in family life; he loved something different, and enjoyed that to the full. 'Take everything you can for yourself, and don't let others rule you; to belong to yourself—that's the whole point of life,' he once said to me. On another occasion, I was playing the role of a young democrat in front of him, and began arguing about freedom (that was one of his 'kind' days, as I called them, and on days like that I could talk to him about anything I liked).

'Freedom,' he repeated. 'But do you know what can give a man freedom?'

'What?'

'Will. One's own will. And it gives you power, which is better than freedom. Learn to exercise your will, and you'll be free, and in command.'

More than anything else, and beyond anything else, my father wanted to live. And live he did . . . Perhaps he had a premonition that he had not long to enjoy 'this thing called life': he died at forty-two. I told him about my visit to the Zasekins in great detail. He listened to me, half attentively and half absently, sitting on a bench and tracing patterns in the sand with the tip of his cane. From time to time he laughed, giving me a bright, quizzical look, or challenged me with a brief question or objection. At first I didn't even dare to pronounce Zinaida's name, but then I couldn't restrain myself and began singing her praises. My father laughed once more. Then he became thoughtful, stretched and stood up.

I recalled that as he came out of the house, he had ordered his horse saddled up. He was a first-class rider, and had known how to tame the wildest of horses long before Mister Rarey.

'Can I come with you, Papa?' I asked.

'No,' he replied, and his face took on his usual look of affectionate indifference once again. 'You go, if you like. Tell the coachman I'm not riding.'

He turned his back on me and walked quickly off. I watched him disappear out of the gate, and saw his hat moving along the fence. He went into the Zasekins' house.

He spent no more than an hour there, but then went straight off to town, only returning in the evening.

After dinner I went round to the Zasekins' myself. I found no one in the drawing room but the old princess. When she saw me, she scratched her head under her cap with the tip of a knitting needle and asked me whether I could copy out a petition for her.

'With pleasure,' I replied, and sat down on the edge of a chair.

'Only be sure to write the letters big,' she said, handing me a dirty sheet of paper. 'Couldn't you do it today, my young man?'

'Certainly, I'll copy it out today.'

The door to the next room opened a crack, and Zinaida's face appeared—pale, pensive, with her hair carelessly swept back. She looked at me with her large, cold eyes and quietly closed the door again.

'Zina! Hey, Zina!' called the old lady. But Zinaida didn't answer. I took away the old lady's petition and spent the whole evening on it.

IX

My 'passion' began that day. I remember feeling rather like a young man about to enter government service. I had ceased to be just a young boy: now I was someone in love. I have said that my passion began that day, but I might have added that my sufferings, too, began that same day. In Zina's absence, I pined for her; my head was empty, nothing that I did came right, and for days on end I thought obsessively about her . . . I pined for her; but when she was there I felt no better. I was jealous, and conscious of my own insignificance, and stupidly sulky, or stupidly servile—and still some invincible force drew me to her, and every time I walked into her room, I could not help trembling with happiness.

Zinaida immediately realized that I had fallen in love with her—it never crossed my mind to hide it— and she made fun of my feelings, led me on, petted me and tormented me. It must be delicious to be the sole source, despotic and arbitrary, of someone else's profoundest joys and deepest miseries: I was like soft wax in Zinaida's hands. As a matter of fact, I was not the only one to be in love with her. All the men who came to her house were madly in love with her, and she kept every one of them on a leash at her feet. She enjoyed filling them with hope and fear in turn, playing with them just as she pleased, like puppets on a string (she called that 'knocking people against each other'); and they all happily submitted and never thought to resist. Her whole lively, attractive personality was an enchanting mixture of cunning and thoughtlessness, artifice and simplicity, tranquillity and mischief. Everything she did or said, every gesture, carried a subtle aura of light-hearted charm, it all conveyed her unique power and playfulness. And her face, too, was always changing, always playful; it reflected a mocking, thoughtful and passionate nature, all in an instant. The most varied emotions, light and fleeting as cloud shadows on a day of sun and wind, constantly chased one another across her lips and eyes.

She needed every one of her admirers. Belovzorov, whom she sometimes called 'my wild beast', and sometimes just 'mine', would happily have thrown himself into the flames for her. With no hopes of winning her by his intellect or other qualities, he yet went on proposing marriage to her and hinting that all the others were mere time-wasters. Maidanov echoed the poetic notes in her spirit: like almost all writers, he had quite a cold personality, but he fervently assured her (and perhaps himself too) that he worshipped her; he extolled her in his interminable verses, declaiming them to her with an ecstasy that was forced and yet sincere. She was fond of him, but made fun of him a bit; she didn't entirely trust him, and after listening to one of his outpourings she would make him read Pushkin to her, to 'clear the air' as she put it.

Lushin, the ironic, cynical-sounding doctor, knew her better than anyone—and loved her more than anyone, though he abused her to her face and behind her back. She respected him, but didn't let him get away with anything, and sometimes took a particular sadistic pleasure in reminding him that he was her slave as well. 'I'm a flirt, I'm heartless, I have the soul of an actress,' she once said to him in my presence. 'So, that's fine! Give me your hand, and I'll stick a pin in it, and you'll be embarrassed in front of this young man—it'll hurt, but you, Sir Truth-teller, will have to laugh it off!' Lushin blushed and turned away, biting his lip, but finally offered his hand. She pricked it, and he really did burst out laughing . . . and she laughed too, pressing the pin quite deep into his flesh and looking into his eyes, while he looked helplessly this way and that . . .

The relationship between Zinaida and Count Malevsky was the one I found hardest of all to understand. He was handsome, sharp and intelligent, but even I, a boy of sixteen, could sense something ambivalent and false in him, and I was amazed that Zinaida didn't see it. Or perhaps she did see that falseness in him, and wasn't put off by it. Her irregular upbringing, her strange acquaintances and habits, the constant presence of her mother, the poverty and disorder of her home—everything, even the very freedom of this young girl's life and her awareness that she was superior to everyone around her, must have combined to instil in her a sort of half-contemptuous, careless indifference. There were times when she would react to anything that happened—Boniface coming in to announce that there was no sugar, or some nasty piece of gossip emerging, or the guests quarrelling—by merely tossing her curls and saying 'what a lot of nonsense!'—she simply couldn't care less.

But I myself would seethe with indignation to see Malevsky sauntering up to her in his sly, foxy way, leaning elegantly against the back of her chair and whispering in her ear with his smug, ingratiating little smile—only for her to fold her arms, give him a searching look, and smile back at him, shaking her head.

'What's the great attraction of receiving Mister Malevsky?' I asked her once.

'Oh, he has such a pretty moustache,' she replied. 'But of course it wouldn't appeal to you.'

'You wouldn't be thinking I love him, would you?' she asked me another time. 'No, I couldn't love anyone I had to look down on. I need someone who can master me . . . But I'll never come across anyone like that, thank heavens! I'm never going to let anyone get his claws into me, certainly not!'

'So you're never going to love anyone?'

'What about you? Don't I love you?' she said, flicking me on the nose with the tip of her glove.

Yes, Zinaida used to tease me a great deal. For three weeks I saw her every day—and what didn't she do with me! She rarely visited us, and I wasn't sorry about that. In our home she would turn into a young lady, a princess—and I felt shy of her. I was afraid of betraying myself to my mother, who was very hostile to Zinaida and kept an unfriendly eye on us. I was not so scared of my father, who seemed almost not to notice me and spoke very little to her, though in a particularly meaningful and intelligent way. I stopped doing any work, or reading anything; I even stopped going for walks or riding. Like a beetle tied by the leg, I circled endlessly round my beloved little lodge; I felt as if I wanted to stay there for ever . . . but that was impossible. My mother grumbled at me, and even Zinaida herself sometimes sent me packing. Then I would lock myself in my room, or go right down to the end of the garden, climb onto the ruins of a tall stone orangery, dangle my legs over the wall facing the street, and sit there for hours on end, gazing and gazing and not seeing anything. On the dusty nettles at my feet, white butterflies flitted idly to and fro; a saucy sparrow perched on the dilapidated red brick-work nearby and twittered crossly, turning his little body constantly this way and that and fanning his tail; the rooks, still suspicious of me, perched high up on the leafless top of a birch tree and cawed from time to time; the sun and the wind played softly over the spindly branches; now and then the sound of the bells of the Donskoy monastery drifted over to me, peaceful and melancholy; and I sat and gazed, and listened, and all my soul was filled with a nameless sensation that embraced everything—sadness, and happiness, and a premonition of the future, and long-ing, and fear. But at the time I understood none of all that; I could never have given a name to any of the thoughts and feelings seething within me, or else I would have called them all by a single name—the name of Zinaida.

Meanwhile Zinaida went on playing with me like a cat with a mouse. Sometimes she was coquettish—and I melted and was filled with anguish; then she would suddenly push me away—and I would not dare to approach her, nor even look at her.

She had been very cold towards me for several days, I remember, and I had altogether lost heart; when I timidly slipped into their lodge, I tried to stay close to the old princess, though she had become very cantankerous and crotchety just at that point—the business of her bills of exchange was going badly, and she had already had two interviews with the local police chief.

One day I was walking in our garden near that same fence—and I saw Zinaida. She was sitting on the grass, leaning on both arms, and not moving. I tried to slip away, but she suddenly raised her head and made a commanding gesture. I froze to the spot, not understanding what she meant. She repeated her gesture and I hopped over the fence at once, and ran joyfully up to her; but she halted me with a look and pointed to the path two steps away from her. Full of embarrassment, and not knowing what to do, I knelt down at the edge of the path. She was so pale, every feature was full of such bitter grief, such profound weariness, that my heart was pierced, and I found myself stammering, 'What's wrong?'

Zinaida stretched out a hand, pulled up a blade of grass, bit it and tossed it away from her.

'Do you love me very much?' she finally asked. 'Yes? You do?'

I didn't answer. What would have been the point?

'Yes,' she repeated. 'That's how it is. The same eyes,' she went on, then fell into thought, covering her face with her hands. 'Everything repels me now,' she whispered. 'I wish I could run away to the ends of the earth . . . I can't bear this, I can't cope . . . And what I've got ahead of me! . . . Oh, I'm so miserable . . . my God, how miserable I am!'

'Why?' I asked timidly.

Zinaida did not answer, but merely shrugged her shoulders. I stayed kneeling there, gazing at her in deepest misery. Every word she spoke had cut into my heart. At that moment, I believe I would have gladly given up my life to save her from her grief. I gazed at her, and—despite not understanding why she was wretched—I vividly pictured to myself how she had suddenly rushed out into the garden, overcome with unbearable sorrow, and flung herself down on the grass as if felled by a blow. Everything around her was light and green, the wind rustled the leaves on the trees, now and then waving the long cane of a raspberry bush over her head. Somewhere, doves were cooing; the bees hummed as they skimmed low over the scanty grass. The gentle blue sky shone overhead. And I felt so sorrowful . . .

'Recite me some poetry,' said Zinaida in an undertone, leaning on one elbow. 'I like it when you recite poetry. You have a sing-song voice, but never mind—you're young. Recite "On the Hills of Georgia" for me. Only sit down first.'

I sat down and recited 'On the Hills of Georgia'.

' "Because the heart's unable not to love",' repeated Zinaida. 'That's what's good about poetry—it tells us things that don't exist, but things that are better than what does exist—and not only that, things that are more like the truth . . . The heart's unable not to love—and it would like not to, but it can't help it!' She fell silent again, then suddenly gave a shiver and stood up. 'Come on. Maidanov is sitting with Mama; he brought me his poem, and I walked out on him. Now he's upset as well . . . what can I do! One day you'll find out . . . only don't be angry with me!'

Zinaida hurriedly squeezed my hand and ran off ahead of me. We went back to the lodge. Maidanov started reciting his recently printed poem 'The Murderer', but I wasn't listening. He was declaiming his iambic tetrameters, droning and shouting; the rhymes jingled, turn and turn about, like little bells, noisy and meaningless, while I just looked at Zinaida and tried to understand what she had meant by those last words of hers.

> *'Or can it be, some secret rival*
> *Has overcome thee in my stead?—'*

Maidanov suddenly cried, in his nasal voice—and my eyes met Zinaida's. She lowered hers and blushed slightly. I saw her blush, and felt a chill of dread. I had been jealous of her before, but it was only at this instant that the thought dawned on me that she had fallen in love. 'My God! She's in love!'

X

That was when my real torments began. I racked my brains, turning the question over and over in my mind, and kept an unremitting watch on Zinaida—in secret, as far as I could. She had changed—that was quite clear. She went out for solitary walks, and stayed out a long time. Sometimes she didn't show her face at all, but spent hours on end in her room. She had never behaved like that before. I suddenly became, or fancied I had become, extraordinarily observant.

'Is it him? Or could it even be him?' I wondered to myself, passing uneasily in my mind from one of her admirers to another. Count Malevsky (though I felt ashamed for Zinaida when I thought of him) secretly seemed to me the most dangerous.

For all my observation, I never saw beyond the end of my nose; and my attempts at secrecy probably deceived no one. Doctor Lushin, at least, soon saw through me. But he too had undergone a change of late. He had lost weight, and although he laughed just as often, it sounded hollow, more curt and bitter. His light irony, his affected cynicism, had given way to an uncontrollable nervous irritability.

'Why do you keep endlessly hanging around here, young man?' he once asked me when we were alone in the Zasekins' salon. (The young princess hadn't returned from her walk, while her mother's shrill voice could be heard from upstairs, swearing at her chambermaid.) 'You ought to be working, you ought to be at your studies, while you're young; what are you doing here?'

'You can't know whether I work at home,' I returned rather haughtily, but in some embarrassment.

'What do you mean, you're working? That's not what's on your mind at all. Still, don't let's argue about it—it's natural at your age. Only you've made a very unfortunate choice. Can't you see what sort of a household this is?'

'I don't understand you,' I said.

'You don't? So much the worse for you. But I consider it my duty to put you on your guard. For someone like me, an old bachelor, it's all right to come here—what could happen to me? Our sort, we've been through it all, you can't hurt us; but you've still got delicate skin. The air's bad for you here—believe me, it could make you ill.'

'What do you mean?'

'Just that. Are you well now? Are you in a normal state? Is it healthy, what you're feeling? Is it good for you?'

'What am I feeling?' I echoed. But I knew in my heart that the doctor was right.

'Oh, young man, young man,' the doctor went on, giving those two words an intonation that seemed very insulting to me. 'What's the use of pretending? You're still at the age when you wear your heart on your sleeve—anyone can read your feelings. Anyway, why go on about it? I'd stop coming here myself, if I . . .' (and the doctor gritted his teeth) '. . . if I wasn't such an odd fish. But here's what astonishes me. How is it that you, an intelligent lad, don't see what's going on around you?'

'What is going on?' I rejoined, tense and on my guard.

The doctor gave me an ironic, pitying look.

'And I'm a fine one myself,' he went on, half to himself; 'as if he needed to be told . . . Anyway,' he added, raising his voice, 'I repeat: the atmosphere round here is no good for you. You like it here—but so what? The air smells good in a greenhouse too, but you can't spend your life there. Honestly, listen to me—go back to your Kaidanov!'

The princess came in and began complaining to the doctor about her toothache. Then Zinaida appeared.

'Here, Doctor,' the princess said, 'you should give her a talking-to. She drinks iced water all day long: is that good for her, with her weak chest?'

'Why do you do that?' asked Lushin.

'Why, what harm can it do?'

'What? You could catch cold and die.'

'Really? You mean that? So much the better, then!'

'So that's how it is!' muttered the doctor. The old princess left the room.

'That's how it is,' repeated Zinaida. 'Do you think it's fun, living like this? Just look around you . . . Good, is it? Do you think I can't understand it? Can't feel it? I enjoy drinking iced water. Can you seriously tell me

I shouldn't risk a life like this one for a moment's enjoyment? Let alone a moment's happiness?'

'Well yes,' remarked Lushin, 'whimsy and wilfulness. Those two words sum you up. Your whole character lies in those two words.'

Zinaida gave a brittle laugh.

'You've missed the boat, my dear Doctor. You haven't got your eyes open, you aren't keeping up. Put on your glasses. I'm bored with whimsy now. Making fools of you all, making a fool of myself—what's the fun in that? As for wilfulness . . . Monsieur Voldemar,' she suddenly added, stamping her little foot, 'don't put on that lugubrious face. I can't stand people feeling sorry for me.' And she walked quickly away.

'It's bad for you, young man, bad for you, the atmosphere round here,' Lushin said again.

XI

That same evening the usual guests gathered at the Zasekins', and I was one of them.

The conversation turned to Maidanov's poem. Zinaida praised it from her heart.

'But do you know what?' she asked him. 'If I were a poet, I'd write about something different. Maybe this is all nonsense, but I sometimes get odd ideas in my head, especially when I can't sleep, in the early mornings when the sky is just beginning to turn pink and grey. For instance, I would . . . You won't laugh at me?'

'No, no!' we all exclaimed with one voice.

'Well,' she went on, folding her arms on her bosom and looking away to one side, 'I'd describe . . . a whole company of young girls, by night, in a big boat—on a quiet river. The moon is shining, they're all dressed in white, with garlands of white flowers, and they're singing, you know, something like a hymn.'

'I see, yes, I see—go on,' Maidanov pronounced in a meaningful, dreamy voice.

'Then, suddenly—noise, laughter, torches, jingling bells on the banks . . . it's a crowd of Bacchantes racing along, singing songs and shouting. Well, it's up to you, master Poet, to paint the picture . . . only I'd like the torches to burn red, with a lot of smoke, and for the Bacchantes to have eyes that glitter under their garlands, and the garlands have to be dark. And don't forget the tiger skins and the goblets—and gold, a lot of gold.'

'Where's the gold supposed to be?' asked Maidanov, tossing back his lank hair and flaring his nostrils.

'Where? On their shoulders, their arms, their feet, everywhere. They say that women in ancient times wore gold bangles round their ankles. The Bacchantes are calling the girls in the boat, to come and join them. The girls have stopped singing their hymn, they can't go on with it; but they don't move. The river carries them to the bank. And now suddenly one of them rises quietly to her feet ... That has to be described well: how she stands up quietly in the moonlight, and how alarmed her friends are ... She has stepped off the edge of the boat, the Bacchantes have surrounded her, and carried her off into the darkness and the night ... Describe the billowing smoke, and the general confusion. All you can hear is their shrieks. And her wreath is left behind on the riverbank.'

Zinaida fell silent. ('Oh! she's fallen in love!' I thought once more.)

'Is that all?' asked Maidanov.

'That's all,' she replied.

'That couldn't be the subject of a long poem,' he declared pompously. 'But I'll use your idea for a piece of lyrical verse.'

'In the Romantic style?' asked Malevsky.

'Yes, Romantic, of course. Byronic.'

'But in my view, Hugo is better than Byron,' opined the young count carelessly. 'More interesting.'

'Hugo is a first-class writer,' replied Maidanov. 'And my friend Tonkosheyev, in his Spanish romance *El Trovador*—'

'Oh, is that the book with the upside-down question marks?' Zinaida interrupted him.

'Yes. The Spanish do that. I wanted to say that Tonkosheyev—'

'Oh, you're going to have another argument about Classicism and Romanticism,' interrupted Zinaida a second time. 'Let's play a game instead.'

'Forfeits?' suggested Lushin.

'No, forfeits are boring. Let's play comparisons.' (This was a game Zinaida herself had invented. Some object was named, and everyone would try to compare it with something else, and whoever thought up the best comparison got a prize.)

She walked over to the window. The sun had just set, and long reddish clouds stretched high across the sky.

'What do those clouds look like?' asked Zinaida, and without waiting for an answer, went on: 'I think they look like those purple sails on Cleopatra's golden ship, when she sailed off to meet Antony. Do you remember, Maidanov, you were telling me about that not long ago?'

We all agreed, like Polonius in *Hamlet*, that the clouds were indeed very like those sails, and that none of us could think of a better comparison.

'And how old was Antony at the time?' asked Zinaida.

'He must certainly have been a young man,' remarked Malevsky.

'Yes, a young man,' Maidanov confidently asserted.

'Pardon me,' exclaimed Lushin, 'he was over forty.'

'Over forty,' repeated Zinaida, casting him a quick glance.

I soon left, and went home. 'She's in love'—my lips formed the words by themselves. 'But with whom?'

XII

Days passed. Zinaida became more and more strange and mysterious. One day I came into her house and found her sitting in a basket chair with her head pressed against the sharp edge of a table. She straightened herself up and I saw—her whole face was wet with tears.

'Oh! it's you!' she said with a bitter smile. 'Just come over here.'

I went up to her. She laid her hand on my head, and suddenly seized hold of my hair and began twisting it.

'That's painful . . .' I eventually said.

'Painful, is it? And aren't I in pain? Aren't I?' she demanded.

'Oh!' she cried out suddenly, realizing that she had pulled out a little tuft of my hair. 'What have I done! Poor Monsieur Voldemar!'

Carefully she straightened out the tuft of hair, wound it round her finger and twisted it into a ring.

'I'll put your hair in a locket and wear it,' she said, with the tears still shining in her eyes. 'Perhaps that'll console you a little . . . and now, goodbye.'

I went back home, where I found an unpleasant scene in progress. My mother was having a row with my father; she was accusing him of something, while he, as always, was preserving a cold, polite silence— soon he left and drove away. I couldn't hear what my mother was saying—besides which, I had other things on my mind. All I remember is that at the end of their argument she had me summoned to her dressing room, where she expressed strong disap- proval of my frequent visits to the old princess, whom she described as *une femme capable de tout*. I kissed her hand (which I always did when I wanted to cut short a conversation), and went to my own room. Zinaida's tears had completely thrown me; I had no idea what to think, and I was on the verge of tears myself— after all, I was still a child, for all my sixteen years. I had given up worrying about Malevsky, though Belovzorov was growing more threatening day by day—he kept looking at the slippery count the way a wolf looks at a sheep. In fact I no longer thought about anything or anyone. I lost myself in my imaginings, and constantly sought out solitary places. I became particularly attached to the ruined greenhouse. I would climb up onto the high wall, and stay sitting there; I was such an unhappy, lonely, miserable youth that I felt sorry for myself—and yet how fond I was of those mournful feelings, how I exulted in them!

Once I was sitting on the wall, gazing into the distance and listening to the bells chiming . . . Suddenly I felt a sensation running through me—not quite a gust of wind, not quite a shiver, but something like a waft of air, an awareness of someone close by . . . I looked down. On the path below me, Zinaida was hurrying past, in a flimsy grey dress and with a pink parasol over her shoulder. She saw me and stopped, pushed aside the brim of her straw hat and looked up at me with her velvet eyes.

'What are you doing, so high up there?' she asked, with an odd smile. 'Look, you keep swearing that you love me—well, if you really love me, jump down and join me here on the path.'

No sooner were the words out than I was flying down as though someone had given me a shove in the back. The wall was about fourteen feet high. I landed on my feet, but I hit the ground so hard that I could not keep my footing. I fell over and briefly passed out. When I recovered my senses, without opening my eyes I could feel Zinaida next to me.

'My darling boy,' she said, leaning over me, and her voice was filled with alarm and tenderness—'how could you do that, how could you obey me like that . . . You know I love you . . . Get up.'

Her breast as she breathed was next to mine, her hands touched my head, and suddenly—what I felt at that moment!—her fresh, soft lips began covering my face with kisses . . . they touched my lips . . . But now Zinaida probably realized from my expression that I had come round, though I still kept my eyes shut—and she quickly stood up and said:

'Well, get up then, you rascal! You mad thing—what are you doing, lying there in the dust?'

So I got up.

'Pass me my parasol,' said Zinaida. 'Just see where I threw it! And don't look at me that way . . . what a lot of nonsense it is! Not hurt, are you? Stung by the nettles, I dare say? Don't look at me, I said . . . But he can't understand a thing, he's not saying a word,' she went on, seemingly talking to herself. 'Now take yourself home, Monsieur Voldemar, and clean yourself up.

And don't you dare follow me, or else I'll be cross, and I'll never—'

She broke off and walked briskly away. I sank down on the path . . . my legs wouldn't carry me. My hands were burning from nettle stings, my spine ached, my head swam; but the sense of bliss that filled me then is something I have never experienced again in my whole life. It lingered as a sweet pain in all my limbs, and eventually resolved itself in little hops and skips and cries of joy. Yes, I really was still a child.

XIII

I was so light-hearted and proud, all that day—I could still feel Zinaida's kisses so vividly on my face, I remembered every word she had spoken with such a shudder of delight, I cherished my unexpected happiness so fondly, that I actually felt scared. I didn't even want to see her, the cause of all these new emotions. I felt that I could ask no more from destiny; that all that was left to me now was to 'take a last deep sigh, and die'.

Next day, however, when I set off to the lodge, I was feeling very embarrassed, and vainly tried to hide the fact under a veneer of modest nonchalance such as would suit a man wanting to show that he knew how to keep a secret. Zinaida greeted me very simply, quite unflustered; she just wagged a finger at me and asked whether I had any bruises. All my modest nonchalance and my air of mystery vanished in an instant, together with my embarrassment. Of course I had not been expecting any special reception, but Zinaida's cool manner was like a pailful of cold water flung over me. I realized that I was just a child in her eyes and that made me very miserable! Zinaida paced back and forth across the room, giving me a quick smile whenever she looked at me; but her thoughts were far away, I could see that clearly . . . 'Should I be the one to say something about yesterday,' I thought, 'ask her where she was going in such a hurry, find out once and for all? . . .'—but I gave up the idea and sat down in a corner.

Belovzorov came in. I was glad to see him.

'I couldn't find a quiet horse for you,' he said sombrely. 'Freitag has one that he'll vouch for—but I'm not sure. I'm uneasy about it.'

'What are you afraid of, might I ask?' said Zinaida.

'What I'm afraid of? Why, you can't ride! Heaven help you if anything happens! What is this crazy idea you've got into your head?'

'Well, that's my business, Monsieur Beast. Then I'll ask Piotr Vasilievich . . .' (Piotr Vasilievich was my father's name. I was surprised to hear her dropping it so lightly and carelessly, as though she were confident that he would do what she wanted.)

'I see,' replied Belovzorov. 'You want to go out riding with him?'

'With him, or someone else—that's none of your business. Not with you, anyway.'

'Not with me,' repeated Belovzorov. 'Just as you like. All right, then, I'll get you a horse.'

'Yes, but mind—I don't want some kind of cow. I'm warning you, I want to gallop.'

'Gallop all you want . . . Who's going with you, Malevsky?'

'Why not him, soldier? Now calm down and stop flashing your eyes at me. I'll take you along with us. You know what I think of Malevsky now—*ffft!*' And she tossed her head.

'You're only saying that to console me,' grumbled Belovzorov.

Zinaida narrowed her eyes at him.

'Does that console you? . . . Oh . . . oh . . . oh . . . you soldier!' she finally said, as if that was the only word she could find. 'What about you, Monsieur Voldemar, would you come out with us?'

'I don't like . . . large parties . . .' I mumbled, keeping my eyes lowered.

'You prefer a tête-à-tête? . . . Well, freedom for the free, and paradise for the . . . saved,' she said with a sigh. 'Go on, then, Belovzorov, get busy. I need a horse by tomorrow.'

'That's all very well,' the old princess interrupted, 'but where's the money to come from?'

Zinaida frowned.

'I'm not asking you for it. Belovzorov will trust me.'

'Trust you, will he . . .' muttered the princess. And suddenly she yelled at the top of her voice: 'Dunyashka!'

'*Maman*, I gave you a little bell,' Zinaida observed.

'Dunyashka!' repeated the old lady.

Belovzorov bowed himself out, and I went with him. Zinaida did not try to keep me.

XIV

Next morning I rose early, cut myself a stick and set out through the town gates. I'll walk off my misery, I said to myself. The weather was beautiful, clear and not too hot; a fresh, lively breeze rustled and frolicked over the fields, so that all the leaves fluttered but nothing was troubled. I wandered far over the hills and through the woods. I was not feeling happy, having left home planning to plunge myself in gloom; but I was young, and the weather was beautiful, and the air was fresh, and I was walking fast, and it was so sweet to lie down and rest alone on the thick grass . . . all that carried the day. Those unforgettable words, those kisses, found their way into my soul again. I enjoyed the thought that Zinaida would have to do justice to my determination, my heroism . . . 'She may like the others better than me,' I thought, 'but so what! The others only talk about what they're going to do, but I did it! And how much more I could do for her! . . .' My imagination took off, and I began picturing to myself how I would save her from her enemies, how I would fight, all bathed in blood, to rescue her from prison, how I would die at her feet. I remembered the picture that hung in our salon: Malek-Adel riding off with Matilda—but now my attention was caught by the sudden appearance of a large spotted woodpecker, busily climbing the narrow trunk of a birch tree and peeping fearfully out from behind it, to right and left, like a musician looking out from behind the neck of a double bass.

Then I sang 'It's not the white snows', and followed that with another romantic song that was popular at the time, 'I await you, when the wanton zephyr'. Then I started declaiming out loud, reciting Yermak's soliloquy to the stars from Khomyakov's tragedy, after which I tried to compose something in a sentimental vein, and even thought up the line that was to conclude my whole poem: 'O Zinaida! Zinaida!' But it didn't work out.

By now it was getting towards dinnertime. I went down into the valley, where a narrow sandy path wound its way towards the town. I followed the path . . . There was a dull thudding of horses' hooves behind me. I looked round, automatically stopping and taking off my cap, and saw my father and Zinaida, riding side by side. My father was telling her something, leaning his whole body over towards her, resting his hand on his horse's neck, and smiling. Zinaida was listening in silence, tight-lipped and with her eyes firmly lowered. At first I could only see the two of them; it was not till some moments later that Belovzorov emerged round a bend in the valley, wearing a hussar's uniform and cape and riding a black horse with foam-flecked lips. This fine horse was tossing its head, snorting and rearing, while its rider at once reined it in and spurred it on. I stood aside. My father gathered up his reins, moved away from Zinaida, she slowly raised her eyes to him—and both galloped off . . . Belovzorov raced after them, clattering his sabre. 'He's as red as a lobster,' I thought; 'and she . . .

why is she so pale? She's been riding all morning, and still she's pale?'

I redoubled my pace, and got home just before dinnertime. My father was already there, changed, washed and freshened up, sitting by my mother's armchair reading the *Journal des Débats* to her in his smooth, resonant voice. But she was paying him no attention, and when she saw me she asked what I had been up to all day, adding that she didn't like people wandering off heaven knew where or who with. 'But I was out for a walk on my own,' I was about to point out—but I looked at my father, and for some reason said nothing.

XV

I saw almost nothing of Zinaida for the next five or six days. She had let it be known she was ill, though that didn't stop her usual visitors from turning up, as they put it, to pay their respects. All, that is, except Maidanov, who always became sulky and dejected if there was no hope of going into raptures. Belovzorov was sitting gloomily in the corner, tightly buttoned and red in the face. Count Malevsky had a constant unfriendly smirk on his thin face; he really was out of favour with Zinaida, and was making great efforts to be obliging to the old princess, riding out in a hired carriage with her to visit the Governor General. Though that excursion had turned out a failure: there had been some unpleasantness for Malevsky, who had been reminded of a scene that had once occurred with some communications officers, and while explaining had been forced to admit that he still lacked experience. Lushin came in twice a day, but did not stay long. I was a little afraid of him after our last heart-to-heart talk, although I felt sincerely drawn to him. One day he went for a walk with me in Neskuchny Park, and was very friendly and nice to me, told me the names and properties of various herbs and flowers, and then suddenly, out of the blue you might say, he struck himself on the forehead and exclaimed, 'Oh, what a fool I was, to think she was a flirt! Some people, obviously, find it sweet to sacrifice themselves.'

'What do you mean by that?' I asked.

'Nothing—to you,' he snapped back at me.

As for me, Zinaida avoided me. My behaviour, I couldn't help noticing, had an unpleasant effect on her. Instinctively, she would turn away from me . . . Instinctively: that was what was so bitter for me, that was what crushed me. But there was no help for it. I tried not to let her see me, but just watched out for her from a distance, not always successfully. As before, something was happening to her that I could not understand: her face had become different, she herself had become different. I was particularly struck by the change I saw in her on one warm, still evening. I was sitting on a low bench under a spreading elder bush; I liked that place because I could see Zinaida's window from there. As I sat there, a little bird fluttered busily around among the dark leaves; a grey cat, stretching its body to its full length, crept cautiously into the garden; the first beetles buzzed heavily around in the clear air, now beginning to grow dark. I sat and looked at the window—and waited to see if it would open. And so it did, and Zinaida appeared there. She was wearing a white dress, and she herself, her face, her shoulders and arms, were so pale they were almost white as well. She stood there motionless for a long time; for a long time she stared motionlessly straight ahead, from under puckered brows. I had never before seen such a look on her face. Then she squeezed her hands tightly together, very tight, lifted them to her lips, to her brow—and then suddenly wrenched her fingers apart, pushed her hair back behind her ears, tossed it free, gave a decisive nod of her head, and slammed the window shut.

Three days later she met me in the garden. I was going to step aside, but she stopped me.

'Give me your hand,' she said, as affectionately as ever. 'We haven't had a chat for ages.'

I glanced at her, with her gentle shining eyes and a smile on her face that I seemed to be seeing through a mist.

'Are you still feeling ill?' I asked.

'No, that's all over now,' she answered, breaking off a small red rose. 'I'm a little tired, but that'll pass too.'

'And you'll be the same as you were before?' I asked.

Zinaida brought the rose up to her face—and I seemed to see the reflection of its vivid petals on her cheeks.

'Why, have I changed?' she asked.

'Yes, you have,' I answered in a low voice.

'I've been cold to you, I know,' Zinaida began, 'but you shouldn't have taken any notice . . . I couldn't help it . . . Anyway, what's the point of talking about it?'

'You don't want me to love you, that's what!' I burst out wretchedly.

'No, you can love me—but not the way you did before.'

'What do you mean?'

'Let's be friends—that's what I mean!' Zinaida let me sniff her rose. 'Look, I'm much older than you. I could have been your aunt; well, not your aunt, but your older sister. You—'

'You just think of me as a child,' I interrupted her.

'All right, then, a child—but a nice, dear, clever one whom I love a lot. Do you know what? I'm appointing you as my page, starting from today. And don't forget: pages have to stick close to their ladies. Here's a symbol of your new dignity,' she added, threading the rose into the buttonhole of my jacket, 'and a token of my favour.'

'There was a time when I had other favours from you,' I muttered.

'Ah!' said Zinaida, giving me a sidelong look. 'What a memory he has! And so? Well, I'm quite willing, right now . . .'

And she bent over and planted a pure, calm kiss on my brow.

I just stared at her. She turned away, saying 'Follow me, my page,' and walked off to the lodge.

I followed her, lost in wonder. Could it be, I asked myself, that this meek, rational girl is that same Zinaida I used to know? Her very walk seemed calmer to me, and her whole figure more stately and graceful . . .

And, my God! how my love burned up again inside me, brighter than ever!

XVI

After dinner the guests gathered in the lodge again, and the young princess came to join them. Everyone was there, just as they had been on that first unforgettable evening. Even Nirmatsky had dragged himself there. This time Maidanov arrived before all the others, bringing a new poem. And we started playing forfeits again, but without the old pranks, the fooling around or the noise. The gypsy quality had gone. Zinaida gave our gathering its new mood. I had the page's privilege of sitting next to her. She had proposed that the person who lost the draw should have to tell his dream; but that was a failure. The dreams either turned out boring (Belovzorov had dreamt he was feeding his horse on carp, and that the horse had a wooden head), or else they were far-fetched inventions. Maidanov served us up a whole romance, with burial vaults, and angels with lyres, and talking flowers, and music borne on the air from afar. Zinaida didn't let him finish.

'If we've moved on to inventions,' she said, 'then let's have everybody tell us some made-up story.'

Belovzorov again found himself first in line.

The young hussar was embarrassed. 'I can't think of anything!' he exclaimed.

'Nonsense!' replied Zinaida. 'Just imagine, say, that you're married, and tell us how you'd pass the time with your wife. Would you lock her up?'

'Yes, I would.'

'And you'd stay by her side?'

'Yes, I'd definitely stay with her.'

'Fine. Well, and then suppose she got bored with that, and was unfaithful to you?'

'Then I'd kill her.'

'But supposing she ran away?'

'I'd chase her and catch her up and kill her anyway.'

'All right. Well, and supposing I was your wife, what would you do then?'

Belovzorov was silent for a while, then:

'I would kill myself.'

Zinaida laughed.

'I can see your story isn't a long one.'

The next forfeit fell to Zinaida. She looked up at the ceiling and pondered.

'All right, listen,' she began at last. 'This is what I've thought up . . . Imagine a splendid palace, a summer night, and an amazing ball. This ball is being given by a young queen. Everywhere there's gold, marble, crystal, silk, lights, diamonds, flowers, incense, every caprice of luxury.'

'You like luxury?' Lushin interrupted.

'Luxury is pretty,' she returned, 'and I like pretty things.'

'More than beauty?'

'Now you're being difficult. I don't understand you. Stop interrupting. So, it's a splendid ball. Lots of guests, they're all young, handsome, brave, and they're all hopelessly in love with the queen.'

'No women among all these guests?' asked Malevsky.

'No. Wait a moment—yes, there are.'

'All ugly?'

'Ravishing. But all the men are in love with the queen. She's tall and graceful. She wears a little gold diadem in her black hair.'

I looked at Zinaida—and in that moment she seemed to stand so far above us all, her pale forehead and steady brows radiated such luminous intelligence and power, that I thought to myself 'You are that queen yourself!'

'They all crowd round her,' Zinaida went on, 'and lavish the most flattering speeches upon her.'

'And does she enjoy flattery?' asked Lushin.

'What an intolerable man! He keeps interrupting . . . Doesn't everyone enjoy flattery?'

'One last question,' said Malevsky. 'Does this queen have a husband?'

'I never even thought of that. No, why should she have a husband?'

'Of course,' echoed Malevsky. 'Why should she have a husband?'

'*Silence!*' cried Maidanov in French, which he spoke badly.

'*Merci*,' said Zinaida. 'So, the queen listens to those speeches, and the music, but she doesn't look at any of the guests. There are six windows, all open from top to bottom, from floor to ceiling, and outside there's the dark sky with big stars, and a dark garden with big trees. The queen looks out into the garden. There, among the trees, is a fountain, a white shadow in the darkness—it rises tall, tall as a spectre. And over the people's voices and the music, the queen hears the water plashing quietly. She looks out and thinks to herself: gentlemen, you are all noble, and clever, and rich, you have all gathered round me and you treasure every word I say, you are all ready to die at my feet, you are in my power . . . But out there, by the fountain, by that plashing water, stands the one who is waiting for me, the one I love, who has me in his power. He is not arrayed in rich clothing, nor with precious stones, no one knows him, but he is waiting for me there and knows that I am coming—and I shall come, and there is no power that could prevent me, when I desire to come to him, and stay with him, and lose myself with him out there, in the darkness of the garden, with the rustling trees and the plashing fountain . . .'

Zinaida fell silent.

'Is that all made up?' asked Malevsky slyly.

Zinaida did not even deign to look at him.

'And what would we do, gentlemen,' Lushin suddenly spoke up, 'if we were among those guests, and knew about the lucky fellow by the fountain?'

'Wait, wait,' Zinaida interrupted him. 'I'll tell you what each one of you would do. You, Belovzorov, you'd challenge him to a duel. Maidanov, you'd write an epigram against him . . . Actually, no, you can't write epigrams; you'd compose some interminable iambic verses in the style of Barbier, and get them printed in the *Telegraph*. Nirmatsky, you'd borrow money off him—no, you'd lend him money and charge him interest. You, Doctor . . .' She stopped. 'You—I don't know what you'd do.'

'As her court physician,' replied Lushin, 'I'd advise the queen not to give balls when she couldn't be bothered with her guests.'

'And perhaps you'd be right. As for you, Count . . .'

'As for me? . . .' Malevsky repeated with his malicious smile.

'You'd offer him a poisoned sweetmeat.'

Malevsky's face twisted for a moment into a Jewish grimace, but then he burst out laughing.

'And coming to you, Monsieur Voldemar . . .' Zinaida went on; 'Anyway, that's enough of that. Let's play at something else.'

'Monsieur Voldemar, in his role as page to the queen, would have held her train as she ran out into the garden,' remarked Malevsky venomously.

I flushed with anger, but Zinaida quickly laid her hand on my shoulder, rose to her feet and said in a rather shaky voice:

'I have never given Your Excellency permission to be impertinent, and therefore I request you to leave us.'

And she pointed to the door.

'Heavens, Princess!' stammered Malevsky, turning pale.

'The princess is right,' cried Belovzorov, rising in his turn.

'I say . . . I never meant . . .' Malevsky went on, 'I don't think I said anything that . . . I never had the faintest intention of offending you . . . I'm very sorry.'

Zinaida glanced frigidly at him and gave him a chilly smile.

'Very well, then, you can stay,' she said with a contemptuous shrug. 'Monsieur Voldemar and I were wrong to take offence. If you enjoy being spiteful, good luck to you.'

'I'm very sorry,' Malevsky repeated once more— while I, remembering Zinaida's gesture, again thought that even a real queen could never have displayed greater dignity than Zinaida when showing an impertinent man the door.

The game of forfeits did not last long after this little scene. Everyone felt rather awkward, not so much from the scene itself, but from a different, not quite definite but yet oppressive sensation. No one spoke about it, but each man could feel it in himself and in his neighbour. Maidanov read us his poem—and Malevsky praised it with exaggerated warmth. 'He's trying to look kind now,' Lushin whispered to me. Soon after that we broke up. Zinaida had suddenly become thoughtful, and the old princess sent word that she had a headache. Nirmatsky began complaining of his rheumatism . . .

I lay awake a long time, troubled by Zinaida's story. 'Could she really have been hinting at something there?' I wondered. 'But who or what was she hinting at? And if there really is something behind it—how can I know what to do? No, no, there can't be anything,' I whispered, turning over from one burning cheek to the other . . . But then I remembered Zinaida's expression as she told her story . . . and remembered Lushin's sudden exclamation in Neskuchny Gardens, and the sudden changes in the way Zinaida treated me, and lost myself in speculation. 'Who is he?' I could see nothing before my eyes but those three words outlined in the darkness, as though there was an ominous cloud hanging low in the sky above me, and I could feel the heavy pressure of it, and was waiting for the imminent cloudburst.

I had recently come to notice a great many things at the Zasekins', and grown used to them all—the messy household, the greasy candle ends, the broken knives and forks, surly old Boniface, the down-at-heel maids, the old princess's own manners—all this strange way of life no longer bothered me . . . But what I could now dimly perceive in Zinaida herself— that was something I couldn't get used to. 'That adventuress' my mother had once called her. An adventuress—she, my idol, my goddess! That epithet burned in my brain, I buried my head in my pillow to escape it, I seethed with indignation—and yet what would I not have consented to, what would I not have given, just to be that lucky man by the fountain!

My blood boiled within me. 'The garden . . . the fountain . . .' I thought to myself. 'I'm going out into the garden.' Quickly I dressed and slipped out of the house. The night was dark, the trees were barely whispering, a cool breeze drifted down from the sky, the fragrance of fennel leaves wafted over from the kitchen garden. I explored all the paths; the light sound of my footsteps both embarrassed me and gave me courage. I stood still, waited, and listened to my heart pounding, quick and hard. At last I approached the fence and leaned against the narrow bar. Suddenly—or had I imagined it?—a female form slipped past me. I stared intently into the darkness and held my breath. What was going on? Was I hearing footsteps—or was that my heartbeat again? 'Who's there?' I whispered almost inaudibly. What was that again? Stifled laughter? . . . or a rustle in the leaves . . . or a sigh, right by my ear? I was scared . . . 'Who's there?' I whispered again, even more quietly.

The air moved for an instant; a fiery streak flashed across the sky—a falling star. 'Zinaida?' I tried to say, but the sound died on my lips. And all around me fell deeply silent, as often happens in the middle of the night . . . Even the grasshoppers in the trees stopped chirruping. All I heard was the chink of a window-pane. I stood and waited, and then went back to my room and my cold bed. I felt strangely excited, as if I had gone to a lovers' tryst, and been left on my own, but had passed close by another's happiness.

XVII

Next day I only glimpsed Zinaida in passing; she was driving somewhere in a cab with the old princess. I did see Lushin, though he barely spared me a greeting; and Malevsky. The young count bared his teeth in a grin, and spoke to me good-naturedly. Of all the men who visited the lodge, he was the only one who managed to get invited to our house and to find favour with my mother. My father had no time for him, and treated him with almost insulting courtesy.

'*Ah, monsieur le page!*' Malevsky began. 'Very pleased to meet you. How is your delightful queen?'

I found his fresh, handsome face so repellent at that moment—and he was looking at me with such a scornfully playful expression—that I gave him no answer.

'Still cross?' he went on. 'You've no reason to be. I wasn't the one who called you a page—and it's usual for pages to wait on queens. But let me point out that you're bad at performing your duties.'

'Why?'

'Pages have to be inseparable from their ladies. They need to know everything the ladies are doing—in fact they ought to watch over them'—he dropped his voice—'day and night.'

'What do you mean?'

'What I mean? I thought I was being quite clear. By day—and by night. By day it doesn't matter much, when it's light and there are people about; but at night—that's when you can expect trouble. I'd advise you not to go to sleep at night, but keep watch—watch as hard as you can. Remember—in the garden, at night, by the fountain: that's where you have to watch. You'll be thanking me.'

Malevsky laughed, and turned his back on me. He probably had not attached any great weight to what he had just said; he had the reputation of a fine creator of mysteries, and was famous for his skill at hoodwinking people at a masked ball—greatly helped by the fact that he was an instinctive natural liar, through and through. He was only trying to tease me; but every word he spoke had flowed like venom through my veins. The blood rushed to my head. 'Aha! So that's how it is!' I said to myself. 'Very well! So yesterday my suspicions were right! And I had every reason to be drawn to the garden. But it shall not be!' I cried out loud, striking my fist against my heart—though I had no idea what it was that should not be. 'Whether it's Malevsky himself who turns up in the garden,' I thought (for perhaps he had given himself away—he was certainly impudent enough), 'or whether it's someone else,' (for the fence round our garden was very low, and anyone could have easily climbed it), 'woe betide whoever it is when I catch him! I wouldn't advise anyone to cross my path! I'll prove to the whole world, and her, the traitress,' (I actually called her a traitress), 'that I know how to have my revenge!'

I went back to my room, opened my desk drawer and took out an English knife that I had bought not long ago. I tried the blade, and scowling with cold, concentrated determination, I slipped it into my pocket—as if such deeds were nothing new or strange to me. My heart was pumping with fury—it felt as if it was turned to stone.

Right up till night-time I kept a scowl on my face, and my lips tight shut; I paced back and forth, clenching my hand round the knife that had grown warm in my pocket, and preparing myself for some dreadful deed. These new, unknown sensations were so fascinating, so delightful even, that I actually did not think much about Zinaida herself. I kept imagining Aleko, the young gypsy—'Whither away, you fine young man?—Lie there . . .', and then 'You are all bathed in blood! What have you done?'—'Nothing!' How cruelly I smiled as I repeated that 'Nothing!' My father was out, but my mother, who had for some time been in a state of almost continuous silent exasperation, noticed my ferocious appearance and asked me at supper, 'What are you glaring at, like a mouse in a meal sack?' I merely replied with a condescending smile, thinking, 'If only she knew!' The clock struck eleven. I went upstairs to my room, but did not undress. I waited till midnight, and finally that struck too. 'Now!' I whispered through gritted teeth, buttoned my coat to the neck, rolled up my sleeves and set off for the garden.

I had already chosen a hiding place to watch from. At the far end of the garden, where the fence between our land and the Zasekins' abutted against a common wall, there grew a lone fir tree. If I stood under the thick lower branches I should be able to see whatever was going on around me, as far as the darkness allowed. And there was a little winding path beside it, which had always struck me as mysterious; it twisted this way and that like a snake, running along the fence which at this point showed traces of having recently been climbed. The path led to a bower of closely grouped acacia trees. I reached the fir tree, leaned against the trunk and began my watch.

The night was as quiet as the one before, but there were fewer dark clouds in the sky, so it was easier to make out the shapes of the bushes and even the taller flowers. For the first minutes of my watch I felt anxious, indeed almost scared. I was prepared to do anything, but wondered what exactly to do. Should I shout out in a thunderous voice: 'Who goes there? Halt! Name yourself, or you're a dead man!'—or should I simply strike the blow? . . . Every sound, every rustle and whisper, seemed loaded with mystery and significance . . . I prepared myself . . . I leaned forward . . . But half an hour passed, and then an hour, and my hot blood calmed and cooled, and I began to be painfully aware that this was all a waste of time, that I was being a bit ridiculous, and that Malevsky had made a fool of me. I left my hiding place and walked all over the garden. As if to mock me, there was not the faintest sound anywhere. Everything was asleep; even our own dog was lying by the gate, curled up in a ball. I climbed up onto the ruins of the greenhouse, looked out over the wide field below, remembered my meeting with Zinaida, and became lost in thought . . .

I gave a start. I seemed to hear the creak of a door opening, then the quiet crack of a snapped twig. In two hops I was back down on the ground—and froze where I stood. There was the clear sound of footsteps, rapid, light but cautious, somewhere in the garden. They were approaching me. 'Here he is . . . Here he is at last!' said my heart. With convulsive haste I pulled my knife from my pocket, and quickly opened it. Glints of red flashed before my eyes, my hair stood on end with terror and fury . . . The footsteps were coming straight towards me, and I bent down and craned forward towards them . . . A man appeared . . . My God! It was my father!

I knew him at once, though he was muffled from top to toe in a dark cape and had his hat pulled down over his face. He tiptoed past without seeing me, though there was nothing to hide me: I had huddled myself up and crouched down so low that I seemed to be almost flat on the ground. Jealous Othello, ready to commit murder, had suddenly turned back into a schoolboy . . . I was so terrified by the sudden appearance of my father that at first I did not even notice where he had come from, or where he had disappeared to. By the time I had straightened up and asked myself 'Why is my father walking about the garden at night?' everything had fallen silent again all around. In my terror I had dropped my knife on the grass, but I didn't even think of looking for it: I was too ashamed. I had sobered up in an instant. On my way home, however, I did go back to my bench under the elder tree and looked up at Zinaida's bedroom window. The small, slightly convex panes showed faintly blue in the dim reflected light of the night sky. And suddenly their light began to change . . . Behind them—I could see, I could see quite clearly—a white blind was being cautiously, quietly lowered, all the way down to the windowsill. And there it stayed, motionless.

'What can it all mean?' I asked aloud. The words came almost unbidden, once I was back in my room. 'A dream? A coincidence? Or . . .' The possibilities that suddenly flooded into my mind were so new and strange that I dared not even entertain them.

XVIII

When I rose next morning I had a headache. All my excitement of the day before had evaporated, to give way to a heavy sense of puzzlement and a sadness I had never felt before—as if something within me was dying.

'What's wrong with you, looking like a rabbit with half its brain taken out?' asked Lushin when we met.

At breakfast I kept casting furtive glances, now at my father, now at my mother. He was calm as ever; and she, as ever, was full of suppressed irritation. I waited to see if my father would strike up a friendly conversation with me, as he sometimes did . . . But he did not even give me his usual cool daily greeting. 'Shall I tell Zinaida everything?' I thought. 'After all, nothing matters any more—it's all over between us.' I went over to see her, but not only did I not tell her anything—I did not even manage to have a conversation with her, as I wanted to. The old princess's son, a twelve-year-old cadet, had arrived from Petersburg for his holidays, and Zinaida immediately put me in charge of her brother.

'Here, Volodia, my dear' (she had never called me that before), 'here's a friend for you. He's called Volodia too. Please be nice to him: he's still a bit shy, but he has a kind heart. Take him to see the Neskuchny Gardens, go for walks with him, take him under your wing. You will, won't you? You're so very kind too!'

She laid both her hands affectionately on my shoulders—and I was completely at a loss. The arrival of this boy had turned me into a boy myself. I looked dumbly at the cadet, who stared wordlessly back at me. Zinaida burst out laughing and pushed us towards each other.

'Go on, give each other a hug, children!'

So we hugged each other.

'Would you like me to show you the garden?' I asked the cadet.

'If you like, sir,' he replied in a typical hoarse cadet's voice.

Zinaida burst out laughing again . . . I had time to notice that she had never before had such a beautiful colour to her face. The cadet and I set off. In our garden we had a little old swing; I got him to sit on the narrow seat and began to push him. He sat there motionless, in his new little uniform of thick cloth with broad stripes of gold braid, holding tightly on to the ropes.

'Why don't you unbutton your collar?' I suggested.

'That's all right, sir, I'm used to it,' he replied, clearing his throat.

He looked a bit like his sister—his eyes in particular reminded me of hers. I enjoyed being kind to him, but that aching sadness was still gnawing at my heart. 'Now I really am a child,' I thought—'but yesterday . . .' I remembered where I had dropped my knife last night, and found it again. The cadet asked to borrow it, picked a thick stalk of lovage, cut it into a whistle and began whistling into it. Othello had whistled too.

But that evening, how he wept, that same Othello, in Zinaida's arms, when she sought him out in a corner of the garden and asked him why he was so miserable. My tears burst out of me so violently that she was alarmed.

'What is it? What is it, Volodia?' she repeated, and when I said nothing and went on weeping, she made to kiss me on my damp cheek.

But I turned away, whispering through my sobs:

'I know everything . . . why have you been making a fool of me?'

'I've wronged you, Volodia . . .' said Zinaida. 'Oh, I've wronged you . . .' she repeated, pressing her hands together. 'What a lot of evil there is in me, and darkness, and sin . . . But I'm not fooling you now, I do love you—you can't even imagine how much, or why . . . But what is it you know?'

What could I say? She stood before me, looking at me—and I was hers through and through, from head to foot, the instant she looked at me . . . A quarter of an hour later the cadet and I and Zinaida were all chasing each other round the garden. I wasn't weeping but laughing, although my swollen eyelids were dropping tears of laughter; instead of my tie, I had Zinaida's hair ribbon round my neck, and I shouted for joy when I managed to catch her round her waist. She could do anything she liked with me.

XIX

I should be hard put to explain what exactly was happening to me in the week after my failed expedition that night. It was a strange, feverish time, a sort of chaos in which the most contradictory emotions, thoughts, suspicions, hopes, joys and sufferings spun around me like a whirlwind. I dreaded looking into myself, if a boy of sixteen is even capable of that; I dreaded facing anything at all, I just rushed to live through each day till evening came. But at night, I slept . . . a childish nonchalance helped me. I didn't want to know whether I was loved, nor want to admit to myself that I was not; I avoided my father, but Zinaida I couldn't avoid . . . In her presence, I burned as if on fire . . . Why should I care what sort of a fire it was that burned and melted me?—it was so sweet to melt and to burn. I surrendered to all my passing sensations, and tricked myself by turning away from my memories, and closing my eyes to what I felt was coming. That state of torment could probably not have lasted long . . . but a thunderbolt fell that put paid to it all in an instant, and hurled me onto a new track.

One day I came home to dinner after a long walk, and heard to my surprise that I would be eating on my own: my father had gone away, and my mother was unwell, did not want anything to eat, and had locked herself in her room. I guessed from the servants' expressions that something extraordinary had happened . . . I dared not question them, but I had a friend, the young waiter Philip, who passionately loved poetry and played the guitar, and I asked him. He told me that my father and mother had had a dreadful scene, and every word could be overheard in the maids' room. Much of it had been in French, but Masha the chambermaid had lived five years with some dressmakers from Paris and understood it all. My mother had accused my father of being unfaithful, on account of his friendship with the young lady next door; my father had begun by denying it, but lost his temper, and then he too said something cruel, 'apparently something about their ages', at which my mother started crying. My mother also mentioned some bill of exchange that he had apparently given to the old princess, and said harsh words about her and about the young lady too. Then my father threatened her.

'And the whole thing happened,' Philip went on, 'because of an anonymous letter, but who wrote it nobody knows, and but for that the whole thing needn't have come out at all, there was no reason why it should.'

'But did anything really happen?' I forced myself to ask, while my hands and feet grew cold and a kind of shudder ran through the depths of my heart.

Philip gave me a meaning wink.

'Yes, it did. You can't hide that sort of thing— though your father was careful this time. You can't manage without hiring a carriage, say, or something like that—and you can't do without the servants either.'

I sent Philip away, and collapsed onto my bed. I did not start sobbing, or give way to despair; I never asked myself when or how this had all happened; I did not wonder why I hadn't guessed at this before, a long time ago—I didn't even blame my father . . . What I had found out now was too much; this sudden revelation had crushed me. It was all over now. All my lovely flowers had been torn out in an instant, and now lay about me, scattered on the ground and trampled underfoot.

XX

Next day my mother announced that she was moving to town. My father came to her bedroom in the morning and stayed alone with her for a long time. Nobody heard what he said to her, but afterwards my mother wasn't crying any more, she had calmed down, and sent for something to eat. But she didn't make an appearance, nor change her decision. I remember that I spent the whole day out of doors, but I never went into the garden and never once looked over to the lodge. That evening I witnessed an astonishing encounter: my father escorted Count Malevsky through the drawing room to the front hall, holding him by the arm, and in the presence of a footman, said to him icily: 'A few days ago, in a certain house, Your Excellency was shown the door. I do not propose at present to enter into any explanations with you, but I have the honour to inform you that if you ever show yourself here again, I shall throw you out of the window. I don't like your handwriting.' The count bowed, gritted his teeth, squirmed, and vanished.

We started making preparations for our move to town, to the Arbat, where we had a house. My father himself probably did not feel like staying in the country any longer. He had managed to talk my mother out of creating a scandal. Everything was done calmly and unhurriedly; my mother even sent word to the old princess to express her regret that her poor health made it impossible to call on her before her departure. I wandered round in a daze, just longing for all this to finish. There was one thought that never left me: how could she, a young girl—and a princess, after all—make up her mind to do something like that, knowing that my father wasn't a free man, when she could easily have married . . . say, Belovzorov? What was she hoping for? Didn't she mind ruining her whole future? Yes, I thought, that's love for you; that's passion; that's devotion . . . And I remembered Lushin's words: 'Some people find it sweet to sacrifice themselves.'

One day I chanced to see a white shape in one of the lodge windows. 'Could that be Zinaida's face?' I wondered. And indeed it was. I couldn't resist: I couldn't part from her without a last goodbye. I waited for my chance, and went over to the lodge.

In the drawing room I was received by the old princess, careless and slovenly as ever.

'What's up, young man, why are your people leaving in such a hurry?' she asked, poking snuff up both nostrils.

I looked at her, and felt a load lifted from my heart. Philip's words about a 'bill of exchange' had been tormenting me. But she suspected nothing—at least it seemed so at the time. Zinaida appeared from the next room, in a black dress, pale and with her hair down. Without a word she took me by the arm and led me out.

'I heard your voice,' she said, 'so I came out at once. And were you going to give us up so lightly, you bad boy?'

'I've come to take my leave of you, Princess,' I replied. 'Probably for ever. You may have heard that we're going away.'

Zinaida looked intently at me.

'Yes, I heard. Thank you for coming. I had been thinking I wouldn't see you again. Don't think badly of me. I haven't always treated you well, but all the same—I'm not the person you think.'

She turned away and leaned against the window.

'Truly, I'm not what you think. I know you have a poor opinion of me.'

'*I* do?'

'Yes, you . . . You do.'

'*I* do?' I repeated sorrowfully, and my heart trembled once more under the spell of her inexpressible, irresistible enchantment. 'I? Believe me, Zinaida Alexandrovna: no matter what you did, no matter how you tormented me, I should love you and adore you to the end of my days.'

She turned quickly round to me, opened her arms wide, took my head in her hands and gave me a warm, passionate kiss. God knows whom that long farewell kiss was meant for, but I greedily savoured its sweetness. I knew it would never be repeated.

'Goodbye . . . goodbye,' I said again and again.

She tore herself away and left the room. I left too. I can't begin to express how I felt as I went. I should not like ever to experience those feelings again; but I would count myself unfortunate if I had never experienced them.

We moved to town. It took some time for me to shake off the past, some time for me to start working again. My wound was gradually healing; and as for my father, I bore him no ill will. On the contrary—he seemed to have grown even taller in my eyes . . . Let the psychologists explain the contradiction if they can.

One day I was walking along the boulevard, and to my inexpressible delight I saw Lushin. I loved him for his directness and his lack of hypocrisy; and besides, he was dear to me for the memories he awoke in me. I rushed over to meet him.

'Aha!' he said, knitting his brows. 'So it's you, young man! Let's have a look at you. You're still looking a bit yellow, but you've lost that nonsense you used to have in your eyes. You look like a man, not a lapdog. That's good. Well, what are you up to? Working?'

I sighed. I didn't want to tell a lie, but I was ashamed to tell the truth.

'Well, never mind,' said Lushin. 'Don't worry. The main thing is to live a normal life, not let yourself be carried away. What's the good of that? Wherever the wave carries you, it's bad; a man has to stand on his own two feet, even if it's on a rock. Here I am, coughing . . . What about Belovzorov, have you heard?'

'No, what about him?'

'Vanished without a trace. They say he's gone off to the Caucasus. Let that be a lesson to you, young man. And it's all because people can't break it off in time, can't get out of the net. Now you seem to have got away unscathed. So watch yourself—don't get caught a second time. Goodbye.'

'I won't get caught . . .' I thought to myself, 'I'll never see her again.' But I was destined to see Zinaida once more.

XXI

My father used to go out riding every day. He had a splendid English chestnut roan horse with a long, narrow neck and long legs. The horse was tireless and bad-tempered, and was called Electric. He would never let anyone ride him but my father. One day my father came to me in a good mood, something I had not seen in him for ages. He was about to ride out, and already had his spurs on. I asked if he would take me with him.

'May as well play leapfrog instead,' he said. 'You'll never keep up with me on your nag.'

'Yes I will. I'll put on some spurs too.'

'Very well, then.'

And we set off. I had a shaggy little black horse, tough and quite mettlesome; it was true that he had to gallop flat out when Electric was going at a fast trot, but even so I kept up. I had never seen anyone ride like my father: he had such a fine, casual, easy seat, it seemed as if the very horse that carried him could feel it and was proud to show him off. We rode along all the boulevards, into the Maidens' Field, jumped a few fences (I was scared to jump at first, but my father despised timid people—so I stopped being afraid), crossed the Moskva River twice, and I was already starting to think that we were on our way home, particularly as he himself had pointed out that my horse was tired, when he suddenly turned at the Crimean Ford and galloped off along the bank. I raced after him. When he reached a great pile of old planks, he leapt briskly down from Electric, told me to dismount as well, handed me his reins and told me to wait for him by the timber. Then he turned down a little lane and disappeared. I walked the horses up and down the riverbank, swearing at Electric who kept tossing his head, shaking himself, snorting and neighing as he walked, and when I stopped he would either scrape his hoof on the ground or whinny and bite my horse on the neck; in short, he behaved like a thoroughly spoilt thoroughbred.

Time passed and my father did not come back. A nasty damp mist was blowing in from the river; a fine drizzle began to fall, spattering a pattern of tiny dark spots over those stupid grey planks nearby that I was so tired of looking at. I was growing really bored, but my father had still not reappeared. A Finnish watchman turned up from somewhere, looking as grey as the planks, with a gigantic old-fashioned shako like a flowerpot on his head, and armed with a halberd (whatever was a watchman doing on the banks of the Moskva?). He came up to me, and turning his wrinkled old face towards me, asked:

'What are you doing with those horses here, young master? Let me hold them for you.'

I did not answer. He asked me for a pinch of snuff. Just to shake him off (and besides, I was in a torment of impatience), I walked away a few paces in the direction my father had taken. Then I went on all the way up the lane, turned the corner—and stopped. Forty paces from me along the street was my father, standing

with his back to me by the open window of a little
wooden house, and leaning in over the windowsill. In
the house, half hidden by a curtain, sat a woman in a
dark dress, talking to him. It was Zinaida.

I was thunderstruck. I had honestly never expected
this. My first impulse was to run away. 'My father will
look round,' I thought, 'and then I'm done for.' But a
stronger emotion, stronger than curiosity, stronger
even than jealousy, held me there. I watched, and tried
to listen. My father seemed to be insisting on something, and Zinaida was refusing. I can still see her face
now—sorrowful, serious, lovely, with an inexpressible
imprint of devotion, sadness, love, and something like
despair—I can't find a better word for it. She was talking in monosyllables, not raising her eyes, and just
smiling a meek, stubborn smile. That smile alone was
enough to bring back my former Zinaida. My father
shrugged his shoulders and straightened his hat on his
head, which was always a sign of impatience in
him . . . Then I heard the words '*Vous devez vous séparer
de cette* . . .' Zinaida drew herself up and held out her
hand . . . Suddenly something unbelievable happened
before my very eyes: my father raised his riding whip,
which he had been using to brush the dust from his
coat-tails—and I heard the sharp crack of the whip on
her bare forearm. I could barely keep from crying out.

Zinaida started, looked wordlessly at my father, slowly lifted her arm to her lips and kissed the red weal that had formed there. My father flung aside his whip, ran hurriedly up the front steps, and burst into the house ... Zinaida turned round, stretched out her arms, threw back her head, and left the window.

My heart sinking with dread, full of amazement and horror, I turned and fled, ran the length of the lane, almost losing my hold on Electric, and returned to the riverbank. I had no idea what was going on. I knew that my cold, self-controlled father could give way to sudden outbursts of fury; and yet I could not make out what it was that I had just seen ... And at the same time I felt that however long I lived, I should never forget that gesture, nor Zinaida's look, nor her smile; I knew that this image of her, this new image that had suddenly taken shape before me, would remain imprinted on my memory for ever. I gazed vacantly at the river, unaware that the tears were pouring down my cheeks. 'He's beating her,' I thought, 'beating her ... beating her ...'

'Come on, then! Give me my horse!' I heard my father's voice behind me.

Mechanically I handed him the reins. He swung himself up into the saddle ... The horse, chilled with standing about, reared up and sprang ten feet forward . . . but my father quickly controlled him, dug in his spurs and punched him on the neck . . . 'Ah, I've got no whip,' he muttered.

I remembered the swish and slap of that same whip a short while back, and shuddered.

'Where did you leave it?' I asked him after a time.

He did not answer, but galloped off. I felt I had to see his face.

'Did you get bored while I was gone?' he asked through clenched teeth.

'A little. Where did you drop your whip, then?'

He gave me a quick look. 'I didn't drop it. I threw it.'

He looked down, lost in thought . . . And just then I saw, for the first and almost the last time, how much tenderness and pity his stern features could express.

He galloped away again, and this time I was quite unable to catch him up; I arrived home a quarter of an hour after him.

'That's love,' I said to myself once more that night, as I sat at my desk on which textbooks and papers were beginning to pile up. 'That's passion . . . How can one not be outraged, how can one put up with a blow like that, no matter whose hand inflicts it—and if it's the hand you love! . . . But it seems you can, if you're in love . . . And there was I . . . imagining . . .'

I had grown up a lot during this last month; and my love, with all its joys and suffering, now struck me as so trivial, and childish, and pitiful, when set against that other, unknown thing which I could barely guess at, which frightened me like an unfamiliar face, beautiful and terrible, which you try in vain to make out in the half-darkness . . .

That same night I had a strange and dreadful dream. I seemed to be entering a dark, low room . . . My father was standing there, holding his whip and stamping on the floor; Zinaida was cowering in the corner, with a red weal not on her arm but on her brow . . . And behind the two of them stood the tall figure of Belovzorov, covered in blood, parting his pallid lips and threatening my father with an angry gesture.

Two months later I entered the university, and six months after that my father died of a stroke. It happened in Petersburg, where he had moved with my mother and me. A few days before his death, he received a letter from Moscow which greatly agitated him . . . He went to ask my mother for something, and apparently he was actually in tears—my father! On the morning of his stroke, he began a letter to me in French. 'My son,' he wrote, 'beware of the love of women, beware of that bliss, beware of that poison . . .'

After his death, my mother sent quite a considerable sum of money to Moscow.

XXII

Some four years passed. I had just left university and wasn't quite sure what to do next, or whose door to knock at. In the meantime I hung around with nothing to do. One fine evening I was at the theatre when I met Maidanov. By now he was married and had entered the service—but I found him unchanged. He still fell into pointless ecstasies and then sudden gloom.

'You know, by the way,' he said, 'Madame Dolskaya's here.'

'Who's Madame Dolskaya?'

'You haven't forgotten, have you? That young Princess Zasekina whom we were all in love with, including you. You remember, out in the country, near Neskuchny Gardens.'

'She married a Dolsky?'

'Yes.'

'And she's here in the theatre?'

'No, but she's in Petersburg. She's just arrived. She's about to go abroad.'

'What sort of a man is her husband?'

'A splendid fellow, with quite a fortune. A colleague of mine in Moscow. You understand—after that business . . . you must have heard all about it,' (Maidanov gave me a knowing smile), 'it wasn't so easy for her to find a husband; there were consequences . . . but with her wits, anything was possible. Go round and visit her—she'll be delighted to see you. She's more beautiful than ever.'

He gave me Zinaida's address. She was staying at the Demut Hotel. All my old memories stirred; and I promised myself that I would pay a visit to my 'old flame' the very next day. But then various things came up, and a week passed, and another, and when I eventually found my way to the Demut Hotel and asked for Madame Dolskaya, I was told that she had died suddenly in childbirth four days earlier.

I felt something like a blow to my heart. The thought that I might have seen her, and had not, and now I never would—that bitter thought gripped me with all the force of an unanswerable reproach. 'Died!' I repeated, staring dumbly at the concierge. Then I silently left the hotel and walked away, I don't know where. Everything that had happened now rose up again before me. So this was what that young, passionate, radiant life had come to in the end—this was what she had been racing towards, full of haste and agitation! Such were my thoughts, as I imagined those dear features, those eyes, those curls—in a narrow box, underground in the damp darkness—in this very place, not far from me who was still alive, and perhaps only a few paces away from my father . . . Such were my thoughts, as I strained my imagination, and yet . . .

Indifferent lips had told me of that death,
Indifferent myself, I heard the tale . . .

Those were the words that echoed in my heart. O youth! youth! You care about nothing, you believe that you possess all the treasures of the world; even sorrow gives you pleasure, even grief amuses you, you are bold and daring, and everything melts in you like wax in the sunshine, like snow in springtime . . . And perhaps the whole secret of your charm lies not in your ability to do whatever you want, but in your ability to believe that you can do it; it lies in the fact that you can cast into the wind forces that could never have served any other purpose; in the fact that each of us seriously regards himself as a prodigal, seriously believes he has the right to say: 'Oh, what I could have achieved, if only I had not wasted my time!'

And I myself . . . what was I hoping for, what was I expecting, what rich future did I foresee, when I had barely a sigh to spare, or a single pang of regret for the phantom of my first love, when it rose for a moment before me?

What had I achieved, out of all I had hoped for? And now that the shades of evening begin to descend over my life, what is left to me that is any fresher or dearer than my memories of that storm which blew over so soon, one springtime morning?

But I am wrong to speak so ill of myself. Even then, in the carelessness of youth, I did not remain deaf to the sorrowful voice that called out to me, the solemn sounds that came to me from beyond the grave. I remember that some days after I heard of Zinaida's death, I myself, obeying some irresistible impulse, was present at the death of a certain poor old woman who lived in the same building as us. Covered in rags, lying on hard wooden planks, with a sack under her head, she died a cruel and painful death. She had spent her whole life in a bitter struggle with daily want; she had never known joy, never tasted the sweetness of honey— how, it seemed, could she not welcome her death, her freedom, her rest? And yet, so long as her aged body still struggled, so long as her breast still heaved in agony under the icy hand that pressed on her, so long as her last strength had not left her, that old woman still continued to cross herself and whisper 'Lord, forgive me my sins'—and it was only with the last spark of her consciousness that the look of dread and terror at her death finally faded from her eyes. And I remember that it was here, by this poor old woman's deathbed, that I became afraid for Zinaida, and wanted to pray for her, and for my father—and for myself.

BEZHIN MEADOW

IT WAS A glorious July day, one of those days that you only ever get when the weather is set fine. The sky is luminous from earliest morning; the sunrise does not blaze like a burning fire, but pours itself out like a bashful blush in the sky. The sun is not fiery or incandescent as it is at the height of a heatwave, nor smoky-red as it is just before a storm, but bright with a cheerful radiance, rising gently below a long, narrow cloud, and shining brightly before hiding itself in the violet mist. Then the fine upper edge of the extended cloud begins to glint with little serpentine shapes, glittering like beaten silver ... And now the dancing beams flash out again—and joyfully, majestically, the magnificent globe of the sun emerges, to rise up as if taking off into the air. Around midday a multitude of high, rounded clouds generally appear, golden-grey with soft white outlines. Like scattered islands in a boundless expanse of flood waters, which flow around them in transparent channels of deep and even blue, these clouds scarcely stir; further off towards the horizon they crowd together so that no blue shows between them, but they themselves have the same azure tinge as the sky itself. They are penetrated through and through with light and warmth. The colour of the horizon, a faint pale lilac, persists unchanged all day, and looks the same on every side; nowhere is there the darkening shadow of a gathering storm, but perhaps to one side or another you may see pale bluish streaks coming down from the sky— showers of almost invisible rain. Towards evening those clouds vanish; the last of them, grey-black and indistinct as smoke, settle as pink billows opposite the setting sun; and over the place where the sun has set, as peacefully as when it rose into the sky, a crimson glow still hangs briefly above the darkening earth. A gentle twinkle, like a cautiously lifted candle, appears in the sky as the evening star comes out. On days like this, all the colours are muted; they are clear, but not bright; everything is marked with a kind of touching modesty. On days like this, the heat can sometimes be intense, sometimes even raising steam from the fields; but the wind disperses and carries off the growing sultriness, while tall white columns of dust devils—a sure sign of fine settled weather—wander along the roads and across the fields. The clear, dry air smells of wormwood, cut rye and buckwheat; even an hour before nightfall, the air does not feel damp. This is the weather the farmer hopes for, when it is time to harvest his wheat.

It was on just such a day that I once went out to shoot grouse in the Chern district of Tula province. I had put up and shot quite a lot of game, and my bulging game bag was cutting cruelly into my shoulder; but by now the evening glow was fading, and cold shadows were beginning to spread and thicken around me. It was still light, though the sun had set and its rays no longer shone through the evening air. Not until then did I at last make up my mind to turn back for home. Briskly I crossed a long patch of scrubland, climbed a hill, and there, instead of the familiar plain I had expected to see, with an oak wood on the right and a little white church in the distance, I found myself facing an entirely different landscape, one that I had never seen before. A narrow valley stretched out at my feet; directly opposite rose a dense aspen wood, like a steep wall in front of me. I stopped, puzzled, and looked around. 'Well!' I thought, 'I must have gone badly wrong. I'm too far to the right.' Surprised at my mistake, I hurried back down the hill. In a moment I was engulfed in a disagreeable stagnant mist, as though

I had gone down into a cellar. The tall thick grass at the bottom of the valley, wet with dew, looked like a flat white tablecloth; walking through it made me feel uneasy. I quickly scrambled up the far side and made my way towards the left, along the aspen wood. The bats were already fluttering over the sleeping treetops, and their mysterious quivering swoops showed up against the dimming light of the sky. High above me, a little falcon sped straight through the air, belatedly hurrying back to its nest. 'Now, as soon as I get to that corner,' I thought, 'the road will be there. But I've gone a good verst out of my way!'

Eventually I reached the end of the wood, but there was no sign of a road. Before me lay a broad stretch of low scrub and unmown grass, and far away in the distance beyond I could see a wide expanse of empty prairie. I stopped once more. 'What's all this? . . . Where can I be?' I wondered. I tried to remember how and where I had walked during the day. 'Ah! That must be the Parakhin scrubland!' I finally exclaimed. 'That's it! And that, over there, that must be the Sindeyev thicket . . . How on earth did I get here? Such a long way . . . Strange! So now I have to bear right again.'

I walked on to the right, across the scrubland. Night was drawing in, gathering close about me like a storm cloud. Darkness seemed to be rising from the ground on all sides with the evening mists, and even drifting down from overhead. I happened upon a little-used, narrow, overgrown path and followed it, peering intently ahead of me. Everything about me had grown dark and quiet—the only thing to be heard was the occasional call of a quail. A small night bird, speeding silently past me low in the air, almost flew into me, and darted aside in fright. I came to the end of the bushes and crossed a field by the hedge. By now I was finding it hard to distinguish individual features; the field was a vague white expanse around me; beyond it, and advancing steadily towards me, was a great mass of gloomy, billowing darkness. My footsteps sounded muffled in the cold air. The sky that had grown pale now began to turn blue again—but this was the deep blue of night. Little stars appeared and twinkled there.

What I had taken for a thicket turned out to be a dark, rounded hillock. 'So where on earth am I?' I repeated aloud, as I stopped for a third time and looked questioningly at my black-and-tan English dog Dianka, beyond a doubt the most intelligent of all four-footed beasts. But this most intelligent of all four-footed beasts merely wagged her tail, blinked her weary eyes despondently, and offered me no practical advice. I felt guilty about her and pressed determinedly on, as if I had suddenly realized where I had to go. Rounding the hillock, I found myself in a hollow, with furrows ploughed all over it. I was suddenly filled with a strange sensation. The hollow was shaped almost exactly like a deep bowl with sloping sides; several tall white stones stood upright at its base, looking as if they had gathered for a secret council. The whole place was so featureless, silent and dumb, and the sky above it looked so dreary, that my heart quailed. From among the stones came the faint, plaintive squeak of some small animal. I hurried back out of the hollow and up the hillock. Until now I had not given up hope of finding my way home, but now I knew for certain that I was completely lost. I gave up trying to recognize my surroundings, almost invisible in the gloom; instead I struck out straight ahead, guiding myself by the stars and going wherever chance would take me. I walked on for about half an hour, though by now my legs would scarcely carry me. Never in my life, I thought, had I been in such desolate surroundings. There was not a glimmer of light to be seen, nor the faintest sound to be heard. One sloping hillside followed another, boundless fields stretched out beyond other fields, and bushes seemed to rise suddenly out of the ground under my nose. I carried on walking, and was preparing to lie down somewhere to wait for morning, when I suddenly found myself on the edge of a terrifying precipice.

My foot was just about to step over it, but I pulled it back. Through the almost opaque darkness of night I could make out, far below me, an enormous plain. A broad river curved around it in a semicircle, flowing away into the distance; here and there a faint metallic glitter, reflected from the water's surface, showed me where it ran. The hill I stood on fell away before me in an almost vertical precipice. Its gigantic outline was black against the blue of the empty air beyond. Directly below me, where the precipice met the plain at its foot, beside the river which here seemed as still and motionless as a dark mirror, I saw the reddish flames and smoke of two little fires burning side by side below the hill. There was a cluster of people milling round them—shifting shadows, with now and then a face glowing in the firelight, a little head with a mop of curly hair . . .

At last I realized where I had got to. That plain was well known in our parts as Bezhin Meadow . . . But I could not possibly return home now, certainly not at night—my weary legs were giving way under me. I made up my mind to go down to those fires, join the people there whom I took to be herdsmen, and wait for daybreak. I got downhill safely, but I had scarcely let go of my last supporting branch when two big shaggy white dogs hurled themselves at me, barking furiously. I heard the shrill voices of children around the fires, and two or three boys jumped up. I answered their shouts of enquiry, they ran up and called off their dogs, which had been very excited at the sight of my Dianka, and I joined them by their fire.

I had been wrong to take the people sitting round the fires for herdsmen. They were just peasant boys from the neighbouring hamlets, guarding a herd of horses. During the summer months in our part of the country, they drive the horses out at night to graze in the open fields, since by day the flies and gnats would give them no peace. Driving the herd out in the early evening and bringing it home again at dawn is a great treat for the peasant boys. Bare-headed and wearing their old fur jackets, they mount the most spirited nags and gallop along, merrily whooping and shouting, swinging their arms and legs, performing high jumps and roaring with laughter. A pillar of fine yellowish dust rises and blows along the road; the thudding hooves can be heard a long way off as the horses race along, their ears pricked. Right in front is a shaggy chestnut horse, with his tail in the air and thistles in his tangled mane, who keeps changing step as he goes.

I told the boys that I had lost my way, and sat down with them. They asked me where I was from, then sat in silence a while, before moving away. We talked a little, then I lay down under a bush nibbled bare by the horses, and looked around me. It was a wonderful scene: a ring of reddish light flickered round the fires and seemed to fade away into the darkness beyond; sometimes the flames burned higher, casting sudden flashes of light beyond the red glow; a narrow tongue of flame would lick at the bare willow twigs, only to vanish; then long thin shadows would appear for an instant, and run right up to the flames. It was a battle of light against darkness. Sometimes, when the flames burned lower and the circle of light closed in, a horse's head would unexpectedly emerge from the surrounding darkness—a bay one with wavy markings, or a white one—and cast us a curious but blank look while hurriedly snatching a mouthful of the long grass beside us, before drawing back and vanishing again. All you would hear was its munching and snorting. From our position in the firelight it was difficult to make out anything in the darkness, so that everything nearby seemed to be hidden by an almost black curtain; but far away towards the horizon one could still make out the long, indistinct smudges of hills and woods. The clear, dark sky hung over us, majestic and inconceivably high, in all its mysterious splendour. My heart felt a sweet sense of oppression as I breathed in that peculiar, fresh and languid fragrance—the fragrance of a Russian summer night. Around me there was scarcely a sound ... save the occasional sudden splash of a big fish, echoing in the river nearby, followed by the gentle rustle of the reeds by the bank as the ripples reached them. Only the flames still crackled quietly.

The boys sat round the fires, and with them those two dogs which had been so intent on gobbling me up. They continued to be uneasy about me for a long time; drowsily blinking and staring into the fire, they sometimes growled with an extraordinary sense of their own dignity—first a growl, then a little whine, as if regretting that they could not indulge their longings.

There were five boys in all: Fedya, Pavlusha, Ilyusha, Kostya and Vanya (I discovered their names from their talk, and now I want to introduce them to you).

Fedya was the eldest; you would have taken him for a fourteen-year-old. He was a graceful boy with handsome, fine and rather delicate features, curly fair hair, bright eyes and a permanent smile, half merry and half abstracted. He looked as if he belonged to a rich family, and had come out to the meadow for fun, not because he had to. He was wearing a brightly coloured print shirt with a yellow border, a new short cloth coat hanging precariously from his narrow little shoulders, and a blue belt with a comb dangling from it. His short boots were obviously his own, not his father's. The second boy, Pavel or Pavlusha, had tousled black hair, grey eyes, prominent cheekbones, a pale pockmarked face, and a large but well-cut mouth; his head was huge ('big as a beer-barrel', as they say), and his body thickset and gawky. He was an unattractive lad, there was no denying it; and yet I took to him, for he had a straightforward, intelligent gaze, and I could hear the force in his voice. His clothing was nothing to boast of—a simple canvas shirt and patched trousers.

The third boy, Ilyusha, had quite a plain, long face, with a hooked nose, short-sighted eyes and an expression of dumb, fretful anxiety. His tight-lipped mouth and furrowed brows never relaxed—he seemed to be constantly squinting into the firelight. His yellow hair, almost white, stuck out in tufts from under his low felt cap, which he kept pulling down over his ears with both hands. He was wearing new bast shoes and foot cloths and he had a length of rope wound three times round his waist, carefully belting in his neat black coat. Neither he nor Pavlusha looked older than twelve.

The fourth boy, Kostya, intrigued me because of his brooding, unhappy look. He had a small, thin, freckled face with a pointed chin like a squirrel's. I could hardly make out his lips, but his large dark eyes with their moist gleam made a strange impression on me, as though they were trying to express something for which a tongue—his own tongue at least—could not find words. His body was small and frail, and his clothes quite shabby.

At first I did not notice the last boy, Vanya: he was lying on the ground, curled snugly up under a square bast rug, from which he only occasionally poked out his curly brown head. He was no older than seven.

I lay under my bush, a little apart from the boys, and watched them. There was a small pan hanging over one of the fires, with potatoes cooking in it. Pavlusha was in charge of it, kneeling down and prodding a splinter of wood into the simmering water. Fedya was lying on the ground, leaning on his elbow, with his coat-tails spread out on either side. Ilyusha was sitting next to Kostya, squinting as intently as before. Kostya's head was drooping a little as he stared into the distance. Vanya was lying motionless under his bast rug. I pretended to sleep. Little by little the boys got into conversation again.

First they just chatted about this and that, tomorrow's jobs, the horses—but suddenly Fedya turned to Ilyusha and seemed to return to an earlier conversation.

'So, did you really see the bogeyman, the domovoy?'

'No, I never did—you can't see them,' said Ilyusha in a hoarse, faint voice, whose tone matched his expression perfectly. 'I heard him . . . And I wasn't the only one either.'

'Where does he live, round your place?' asked Pavlusha.

'In the old roller shed.'

'What? Do you go to the factory, then?'

''Course we do. Me and my brother Avdyushka, we're paper-glazers.'

'Just look at you—factory workers!'

'Well then,' asked Fedya, 'how did you come to hear him?'

'You see, Avdyushka and me, and Fyodor Mikheyevsky, and Ivashka Kosoy, and the other Ivashka from Red Hills, and Ivashka Sukhorukov, and some other boys—about ten of us altogether, the whole shift— it turned out we were spending the night in the roller room. Not that it turned out, exactly—it was Nazarov the foreman who made us: "What's the point of you dragging yourselves home, boys," he says, "there's lots to do tomorrow, just you stay here, boys, don't go home." So we stayed behind, and there we all were, lying there together, and Avdyushka says, "What if the domovoy comes? . . ." and he'd only just finished saying that when somebody started walking about overhead; we were all downstairs, and the other one was walking about upstairs, where the wheel is. We could hear him walking, and the floorboards bending and creaking under his weight; and he walked right above our heads, and suddenly we could hear water splashing onto the wheel, really noisy, and the wheel knocked and bumped and started turning, though the sluice covers had been let down. So we wondered who could have raised them and opened the sluices again, and let the water through; and the wheel turned and turned a bit, and then it stopped. And then that other one went to the upstairs door, and started coming down, taking his time; and the steps were really groaning under his feet . . . So then he reached our door, and waited and waited—and suddenly the door burst wide open. We were scared stiff, but when we looked, there was nothing there . . . And then while we watched, we saw the net by one of the vats moving, and it went up in the air, and dipped itself into the vat, and waved this way and that in the air as if someone was rinsing it, and then it went back to its place. And then a hook lifted itself off its nail beside another vat, and then it hung itself back again; and then somebody seemed to come up to the door, and coughed and choked, just like a sheep, but so loud! And we all fell down and huddled together ... Gosh, weren't we scared that time!'

'Well I never!' said Pavel. 'What was he coughing for?'

'I don't know. Perhaps it was damp.'

Nobody spoke for a bit.

'Anyway,' said Fedya, 'are the potatoes done?'

Pavlusha felt them.

'No, they're still raw ... My, what a splash,' he added, looking over to the river. 'Must have been a pike ... And there's a falling star.'

'Now listen to what I'm going to tell you, boys,' said Kostya in a thin little voice. 'Here's what my dad was telling me the other day.'

'Well, go on,' said Fedya condescendingly.

'You know Gavrila, the carpenter in the big village?'

'Yes, go on.'

'But do you know why he's always so miserable, never says anything, I mean? Here's why he's so miserable. One day he went, my dad was saying, he went into the forest to pick nuts. So he went to the

forest for nuts, and he lost his way, and ended up God
knows where. And he walked on and on, boys, but it
was no good, he couldn't find the path, and the night
was coming. So he sat down under a tree; let's wait
for morning, he thought; so he sat down and fell
asleep. So he was sleeping, when he suddenly heard
someone calling him, and he looks up, but nobody's
there. He fell asleep again, and the calling came
again. So he looks and looks again, and there's a
wood sprite, a russalka, on a branch in front of him,
rocking herself and calling him to come to her, and
she's killing herself laughing and laughing . . . And
the moon was shining bright, so bright, it was so
clear, he could see everything, boys. And she's calling
him, and she was so bright and shining herself, sitting
on the branch, all white, like a roach or a dace, or a
carp can be that silvery-white as well . . . Gavrila the
carpenter, he almost fainted right away, brothers, but
she went on laughing and kept beckoning him over,
to come to her . . . Gavrila was just about to get up
and do what she wanted, but the Lord must have told
him what to do, and he made the sign of the cross . . .
Only how hard it must have been to cross himself:
well, boys, he says his hand was like a stone, it
wouldn't move . . . What a man! . . . So as soon as he
crossed himself, that russalka stopped laughing, and

then she suddenly burst out crying . . . She's crying there, brothers, and wiping her eyes with her hair, and her hair's just as green as that hemp. So Gavrila, he looks at her, and he looks at her, and he asks her: "What are you crying for, you bit of forest greenery?" But the russalka, she tells him: "You never should have crossed yourself, you human being you, you could have lived merrily with me till the end of your days; but now I'm weeping broken-hearted because you crossed yourself. But I'm not the only one—now you'll be broken-hearted yourself, till the end of your days." And then, boys, she vanished, and that same moment Gavrila could see his way out of the forest . . . But ever since then he's been miserable, wherever he goes.'

'Think of that!' Fedya mused after a while. 'How could such a wicked forest creature ruin a Christian soul? When he hadn't even obeyed her?'

'Yes, just think!' agreed Kostya. 'And Gavrila said she had such a sad, thin little voice, just like a toad.'

'Did your father tell you all that himself?' Fedya asked.

'Yes, I was lying on my bunk, and I heard it all.'

'How strange! What's he got to be miserable about? . . . But she must have fancied him, if she beckoned him to come to her.'

'Yes—fancied him indeed!' Ilyusha broke in. 'So she did—she wanted to tickle him to death, that's what! That's what they do, those russalkas.'

'But there must be russalkas round here too,' remarked Fedya.

'No,' said Kostya, 'this is a clear, open place. Except for one thing—the river's too close.'

Everyone was silent. Suddenly, from somewhere in the distance, there came a long-drawn-out, echoing, almost wailing sound, one of those mysterious night sounds that sometimes break in on a deep quietness, rising and hanging in the air, and then fade and seem to die away. You strain your ears, and there seems to be nothing there, but your ears are still ringing. It felt as if someone had uttered a long, long cry, right over by the horizon, and someone else in the forest had called back in a shrill, high-pitched laugh, and then a faint whistling hiss had sounded along the river. The boys looked at one another and shivered . . .

'The holy powers be with us!' whispered Ilyusha.

'Hey, you brave ravens!' cried Pavel. 'What are you so scared of? Just look, the potatoes are ready!' Everybody gathered round the pot and began eating the steaming potatoes; only Vanya didn't stir. 'What's the matter?' asked Pavel. But the boy wouldn't come out from under his rug, and soon the pot was empty.

'Boys, did you hear what happened at Varnavitsi the other day?' asked Ilyusha.

'Up at the dam?' said Fedya.

'Yes, yes, at the dam, the broken one. That's an unclean place all right, such a haunted place, and so lonely. All those pits and gullies everywhere, and they're all full of snakes.'

'So what happened? Go on, tell us!'

'Here's what. Fedya, maybe you don't know this, but there's a drowned man buried there; he drowned long, long ago, when the pond was still deep, and you can still see his grave there, but you can only just make it out—just a little mound like this . . . Well, a few days ago, the bailiff calls Yermil the kennelman, and says, "Yermil, go for the post." Now it's always Yermil who goes to the post for us; he's let all his dogs die, they never live long with him for some reason, never have done, but he's a good kennelman, everyone knows that. So Yermil set off for the post, and he was a long time in town, and when he rode back he was drunk. It was night, a bright moonlit night . . . So Yermil rode back over the dam, that was the way he had to go. So there he is, Yermil the kennelman, riding across it, and he sees a little lamb walking around on the drowned man's grave, all white and curly, a dear little thing. So Yermil, he thinks, "I'll take him along—no point leaving him there to die," so he gets off his horse, and picks the lamb up in his arms . . . And that lamb, he doesn't mind. So Yermil walks back to his horse, and the horse rears up away from him, and snorts, and tosses his head; but he says "Whoa, boy," and gets up with the lamb in his arms, and sets off again, holding the lamb in front of him. And he's looking at the lamb, and the lamb's staring back, straight in his eyes. And Yermil the kennelman, he comes over all queer, "I've never known a lamb stare in a man's eyes like this," he thinks; but never mind, he begins stroking that lamb on his woolly fleece, like this, and says to him: "There, there, lambkin!"—and the lamb, he suddenly bares his teeth and says it back to him: "There, there, lambkin!"'

No sooner had the storyteller spoken those words than both dogs leapt up, rushed away from the fire barking frantically, and vanished into the dark. All the boys were alarmed. Vanya started out from under his rug. Pavlusha yelled and raced off after the dogs. Their barking grew fainter in the distance . . . Then came the sound of galloping hooves—the herd of horses had taken fright. Pavlusha was shouting 'Hey there, Grey! Zhuchka!' and a few moments later the barking stopped, and by now Pavlusha's voice was coming from far away. Some time passed. The boys were looking at each other anxiously, waiting to see what would happen . . . Suddenly there was the sound of a horse galloping, and it drew up right by the bonfire. Pavlusha seized hold of its mane and sprang nimbly off. Both dogs leapt into the circle of light and sat straight down with their red tongues hanging out.

'What was it? What's happened?' asked the boys.

'Nothing,' replied Pavel, gesturing at his horse. 'The dogs just scented something. A wolf, I expect,' he added indifferently, though he was still panting.

I could not help admiring him. He was looking very fine just then. His ugly face, animated by the chase, was all aglow with daring courage and firm resolution. Without even a stick in his hand, he had not hesitated to gallop off alone in the darkness to face a wolf . . . 'What a splendid lad!' I thought as I looked at him.

'Did you see any wolves, then?' asked timid little Kostya.

'There's always lots of them about,' said Pavel, 'but they only bother you in the winter.'

And he snuggled down by the fireside again. As he was sitting down, he laid a hand on the shaggy head of one of the dogs, and the delighted animal held its head still for a long while, gazing proudly and gratefully at Pavlusha out of the corner of its eye.

Vanya huddled down under his rug once more.

'What scary tales you were telling us, Ilyusha,' remarked Fedya, who as the son of a rich peasant found himself leading the conversation (though he himself did not say much, as though afraid of lowering his dignity). 'And what the devil came over those dogs, to set them off barking? . . . But that's right, I've been told that place of yours is haunted.'

'Varnavitsi? I should say it is! They say the old master has been seen there lots of times, the dead landowner. They say he walks around in a long kaftan, and keeps sighing and searching for something on the ground. Grandpa Trofimich met him once, "Ivan Ivanich," he says, "what are you looking for there on the ground?"'

'He asked him that?' interrupted Fedya in amazement.

'Yes, he did.'

'Well, what a man, that Trofimich! . . . So, what did the other one say?'

'"The enchanted herb that opens locks," he says, "that's what I'm looking for." Says it in such a deep, hollow voice: "The enchanted herb".—"What do you want it for, Ivan Ivanich, the enchanted herb?"—"My tomb is pressing down on me, Trofimich. I want to get out, out of there . . ."'

'Just think!' said Fedya, 'He can't have had much of a life.'

'What a miracle!' said Kostya. 'I thought you could only see dead people on All Hallows.'

'You can see dead people any time,' Ilyusha returned confidently. As far as I could see, he knew all the country superstitions better than the other boys. 'But on All Hallows you can see living people too, I mean the ones who are going to die that year. All you have to do is sit down that night in the church porch and keep your eyes on the road. Those people will walk by you along the road, the ones who are going to die that year. Last year in our village, Baba Ulyana went there.'

'Well, and did she see anyone?' asked Kostya eagerly.

''Course she did. First of all she just sat there a long, long time, without seeing or hearing anyone . . . except that there seemed to be a little dog, barking on and on somewhere . . . And suddenly she looks, and there's a boy coming along the road, in just his shirt. So she looked to see, and it was Ivashka Fedoseyev walking by . . .'

'The one who died in the spring?' asked Fedya.

'The very same. Walked past, never lifted his head . . . But Ulyana recognized him . . . And then she went on looking, and an old woman was coming. So she peered and peered at her, and oh my Lord! it was herself walking along the road, Ulyana herself.'

'You don't mean it was herself?'

'I swear it was, her own self.'

'But what . . . I mean, she hasn't died yet?'

'No, but the year isn't out. Just look at her. Her soul's barely clinging on to her body.'

Everybody fell silent. Pavel threw a handful of dry twigs onto the fire. Instantly the flames burned up, the twigs blackened in a trice, crackling and smoking and twisting in the fire and raising their burning tips in the air. A flickering glow shone out in all directions, especially upwards. And suddenly, heaven knows where from, a little white dove flew straight into the glowing light, fluttered round and round in terror, bathed in light, and vanished with a flapping of its wings.

'Can't find its home, I expect,' said Pavel. 'Now it'll carry on till it flies into something, and wherever that is, it'll spend the night there till dawn comes.'

'But Pavlusha,' said Kostya, 'mightn't that have been a blessed soul flying up to heaven, eh?'

Pavel threw another handful of twigs onto the fire.

'Could be,' he said at last.

'But tell me, Pavlusha,' began Fedya, 'did you at Shalamovo see that heavenly apparition too?'

'What, when the sun disappeared? Of course we did.'

'I guess you were all frightened too?'

'It wasn't just us. Our master warned us beforehand that there'd be a heavenly apparition, but even so, when it got dark, they say he was terrified right out of his wits. And the old cook woman in the house serfs' hut, the moment it got dark, do you know, she grabbed the oven tongs and smashed every one of the pots in the oven. "None of us will ever eat again," she says, "the last day has come." And there was soup running all over the place. And in our village, people were saying there'd be white wolves running wild over the earth, eating people, and a bird of prey would come down on us, or they might even catch sight of Trishka himself.'

'Who's this Trishka?' asked Kostya.

'Don't you know?' replied Ilyusha heatedly. 'Well, boy, wherever have you been, if you don't even know Trishka? Don't any of your lot ever leave your village, then? I mean . . . Trishka—he's an extraordinary man, and he's going to come, he'll come when it's the last days. And he'll be such an extraordinary man that no one will be able to catch him, nor they won't be able to do anything to him, that's how extraordinary he'll be.

Say the Christian folk set out to catch him, and they come with sticks and surround him, well, he'll make them look the other way, and while he's distracting them, they'll start fighting each other. Or suppose they put him in prison, say—he'll ask for some water in a bowl, and they'll bring him a bowl of water, and he'll dive into it and they'll never see him again. Or they'll chain him up, and he'll clap his hands and the chains'll fall off him. Anyway, this Trishka will be walking through the villages and the towns, and he's a cunning fellow, this Trishka, and he'll tempt the Christian people . . . and no one will be able to do anything to him . . . That's what an extraordinary, cunning man he'll be.'

'That's right,' Pavel took him up, in his unhurried voice, 'that's what he's like. And our villagers were all expecting him. The old men were saying that as soon as the heavenly apparition begins, that's when Trishka will turn up. And then the heavenly apparition began. And everyone poured out onto the streets and into the fields, and waited to see what would happen. You know how the land round our parts is all open country. They're looking, and suddenly there's a man walking down the hill from the hamlet on top, such a peculiar man, with a very odd head . . . And everybody burst out shouting "Look, Trishka's coming! Look, Trishka's coming!" and rushed off in all directions. Our village headman crept into a ditch, and his wife got stuck under their gate and she's yelling her head off, she frightened their guard dog so badly that it slipped its chain and jumped the fence and ran off into the forest; and Kuzka's father Dorotheich jumped into a pile of oats and squatted down and started squawking like a quail. "Perhaps," he thinks, "the Great Enemy, the Destroyer of Souls, will take pity on a bird." Everyone was in such a state! . . . But the man walking downhill, that was our cooper Vavila: he'd just bought himself a new pitcher, and he was carrying the empty pitcher on his head.'

All the boys laughed, and then they were silent for a bit, which often happens when people have been having a conversation in the open air. I looked round. The night was deep, majestic and solemn; the cool damp late evening had given way to the dry warmth of midnight, which would hang for many hours yet like a soft curtain over the sleeping fields. There was still a long time to go before the first lisping sounds, the first rustles and whispers of the morning, and the first dewdrops of daybreak. There was no moon in the sky—it rose late at that time. Countless golden stars seemed to be drifting quietly towards the Milky Way, twinkling one after another; and watching them, you

truly seemed to feel aware of the earth's own relent-
less, headlong rush through space . . .

Suddenly a strange, sharp, painful cry sounded
twice in succession over the river; a few moments later
it came again from further off . . .

Kostya shuddered. 'What was that?'

'That's a heron's cry,' said Pavel coolly.

'A heron . . .' repeated Kostya. 'And what do you
think, Pavlusha—I heard something last night,' he
went on after a brief pause, 'and I thought you might
know . . .'

'What did you hear?'

'Here's what. I was walking from Stony Ridge to
Sashkino, and first I went through our walnut wood,
and then I crossed the meadow—you know, where it
takes a sharp bend, and goes down to a pit full of
water, you know, where it's all overgrown with rushes.
Well, I went on past that pit, boys, and suddenly something in there gave a groan, it was so pitiful, so pitiful—oo-oo . . . oo-oo . . . oo-oo! I was so scared, boys,
I mean, it was late, and that voice was so miserable—I
think I could have cried myself . . . What could that
have been, eh?'

'That was the pit where the robbers drowned Akim
the forester, last summer,' remarked Pavlusha. 'Maybe
it was his soul lamenting.'

'Oh my, boys,' said Kostya, opening his large eyes even wider. 'I'd no idea Akim was drowned in that pit. I'd have been twice as scared!'

'But then people say there are tiny little frogs, too, that cry sadly like that.'

'Frogs? No, no, that wasn't frogs . . . No way . . .' (The heron over the river gave another cry.) 'Just listen to that!' Kostya exclaimed. 'You'd think it was a leshy, a wood spirit, shrieking.'

'No, the leshy doesn't shriek, he's dumb,' Ilyusha interrupted, 'all he does is clap his hands and rattle the branches.'

'So you've seen the leshy, have you?' Fedya asked sarcastically.

'No, I haven't, and God save me from seeing him— but some people have. Just a few days ago, he led one of our peasants astray, set him wandering this way and that through the forest, and round and round the same clearing . . . he never got home till nearly dawn.'

'Well, and did he see him?'

'Yes he did. He's a huge, tall creature, he said, standing there all dark, muffled up in something, as if he's hiding behind a tree, and you can't make him out, for he seems to be hiding from the moon; and looking at you, looking with those huge eyes, and winking, and winking . . .'

'Oh no!' exclaimed Fedya, with a little shudder and a twitch of his shoulders. 'Ugh!'

'What makes all these foul creatures breed in our world?' Pavel wondered. 'Honestly, I can't understand it!'

'Don't speak ill of him—watch out, he'll hear you,' said Ilyusha.

Another silence fell.

'Look up, boys, look up there!' came Vanya's childish voice suddenly. 'Look at God's stars—like a swarm of bees!'

He poked his fresh little face out from under his rug, leaned on his fist and slowly raised his large, soft eyes heavenwards. All the boys looked up at the sky, and a long time passed before they lowered them again.

'Vanya,' began Fedya in a gentle voice, 'how's your sister Anyutka? Is she well?'

'Yes, she's well,' replied Vanya with a slight lisp.

'Ask her—why doesn't she come to see us any more?'

'I don't know.'

'You tell her to come and see us.'

'All right.'

'Tell her I'll give her a treat.'

'Will you give me one too?'

'Yes, you too.'

Vanya sighed. 'No, you don't have to give me one. Better let her have one, she's so nice and kind.'

And Vanya laid his head down on the ground again. Pavel stood up and picked up the empty pan.

'Where are you off to?' Fedya asked him.

'The river, to get some water. I want a drink.'

The dogs got up and followed him.

'Careful not to fall in the river!' Ilyusha called after him.

'Why would he fall in?' said Fedya. 'He'll be careful.'

'Yes, of course he'll be careful; but anything can happen. He could bend down and start scooping up water, and a river fairy, a vodyanoy, could grab him by the arm and pull him in. And then people would say, the lad fell into the water . . . but he never fell in at all . . . Hark at that—he's gone into the reeds,' he added, listening hard.

And indeed the reeds were 'shushing', as people call it, where they were being parted.

'And is it true,' asked Kostya, 'that mad Akulina lost her wits the day she fell into the water?'

'Yes, that was when it happened . . . Just look at her now! But they say she was a great beauty before that. The vodyanoy bewitched her. He can't have expected her to be pulled out so quickly. But while he had her at the bottom of the river, that's when he bewitched her.'

(I had occasionally met Akulina myself. Dreadfully thin, covered in rags, her face black as soot, a dull look in her eyes and teeth always bared, she stands on the roadway stamping her feet on one spot for hours on end, pressing her bony hands hard against her breast and slowly shifting from one leg to the other, like a wild animal in a cage. She understands nothing that is said to her, but just giggles fitfully from time to time.)

'And they say,' Kostya went on, 'Akulina threw herself into the river because her lover had been untrue to her.'

'That's right.'

'And do you remember Vasya?' Kostya added mournfully.

'Which Vasya?' asked Fedya.

'The one that drowned,' said Kostya, 'in this same river. Oh, what a boy he was! Really, what a boy he was! His mother, Feklista, how she loved him, that Vasya! And she seemed to have a feeling, Feklista did, that the water would do for him somehow. Sometimes Vasya would come out with us boys in the summertime, to have a swim in the river, and she'd be all of a tremble! The other women would be fine, coming by with their pails, waddling along, but Feklista would put down her pail and start calling him, "Come back! Come back home, light of my life! Oh, do come back, my little falcon!" And how he happened to drown, the Lord alone knows. He was playing on the bank, and his mother was there too, raking hay, and suddenly she heard a noise as if someone was blowing bubbles through the water—and she looked, and all she could see was Vasya's little cap floating on the water. And ever since then, Feklista hasn't been quite right in the head either; she'll go and lie down at the same spot where he drowned, she'll lie down, boys, and start singing a song—you know, Vasya used to sing that song, and she'll start singing it herself, and she's crying and crying, and complaining bitterly to God . . .'

'Here's Pavlusha back,' said Fedya.

Pavlusha came up to the fire with the pan full of water.

'Listen, boys,' he said after a pause. 'Something bad happened.'

'What is it?' asked Kostya quickly.

'I heard Vasya's voice.'

Everyone shivered.

'What do you mean? What do you mean?' stammered Kostya.

'Honestly, I did. Just as soon as I bent over the water, suddenly I heard Vasya's voice calling me, and it seemed to be coming from under water: "Pavlusha! Pavlusha!" Then I listened some more, and it called me again, "Pavlusha, come here!" So I ran away. But I did get some water.'

'Oh my Lord! Oh my Lord!' said all the boys, and crossed themselves.

'You know, that was the vodyanoy calling you, Pavel,' said Fedya. 'And we were just talking about him, about Vasya.'

'Oh dear, that's a bad sign,' said Ilyusha slowly.

'Well, never mind! Forget it!' said Pavel firmly, and sat down. 'You can't escape your fate.'

The boys became subdued; it was obvious that Pavel's account had moved them deeply. They began to settle down round the fire as if preparing to sleep.

'What's that?' Kostya asked suddenly, raising his head.

Pavel listened.

'That's curlews flying, and whistling.'

'Where are they flying to?'

'The place where they say winter never comes.'

'Why, is there a place like that?'

'Yes, there is.'

'Is it far?'

'Yes, far, far away, over the warm seas.'

Kostya sighed and closed his eyes.

Over three hours had passed since I had joined the boys. The moon had risen at last, though I did not notice it at first, it was such a thin little crescent. This moonless night seemed just as splendid as it had been before . . . But many of the stars that had so recently shone high in the sky had by now descended to the earth's dark edge; everything around us had fallen quite still, as generally only happens in the early mornings; everything was wrapped in the deep, unmoving sleep that comes just before dawn. The air no longer held its powerful fragrance—dampness seemed to be flooding it again. Those short summer nights! And the boys' conversation had faded away like their fires . . . Even the dogs were dozing; and the horses, as far as I could make them out in the faint, glimmering starlight, were also sleeping, with drooping heads . . . I was overcome with a pleasant drowsiness that soon passed into sleep.

A fresh breeze wafted over my face. I opened my eyes: morning was near. There was no dawn blush in the sky yet, but the east had already grown pale. I could see everything around me, though only indistinctly. The pallid grey sky was luminous, cold, with a tinge of blue; the stars now shone with a feeble, flickering light, then vanished altogether. The earth was damp, the leaves sweating with dew; there were living sounds to be heard, and voices; and a little morning breeze was playing restlessly over the fields. My body responded to it with a light, happy shiver. I stood up briskly and walked over to the boys. They were all sleeping like the dead, around their smouldering bonfire. Pavel alone sat up and looked at me intently.

I nodded to him and set off for home along the misty river. I had scarcely gone a couple of versts when I already found myself enveloped in a flood of light— first a crimson glow, then red, then golden streams of warm, youthful radiance: they flowed over the broad, dewy meadow around me, and ran from woodland to woodland over the green hills ahead of me and the long dusty road behind me, and over the bushes glittering in the rosy light of dawn, and along the river that shone with such a shy tinge of blue under the rising mist. Everything stirred, woke, sang, rustled, spoke aloud. Big dewdrops gleamed all round me, like glittering diamonds. Pure and clear, as though washed in the morning coolness, came the notes of a bell. And suddenly the herd of horses, fresh after their night's rest, came galloping past, driven by those same boys whom I knew.

I have to add that, sadly, Pavel died that same year. He was not drowned, but killed by a fall from a horse. Such a shame—he was a splendid lad!

BIRYUK

ONE EVENING I was on my way home from the
hunt, on my own, driving a racing droshky.
There were still some eight versts to go; my fine mare
raced bravely along the dusty road, pricking up her
ears and snorting from time to time; my weary dog ran
along behind, never dropping back a step, as if he was
tethered to the rear wheels. A storm was on the way.
Ahead of us, a gigantic purple storm cloud loomed
over the forest, while long grey clouds scudded overhead, advancing towards me. Willow leaves trembled
and whispered restlessly. All of a sudden the stifling
heat gave way to moist, cool air, as the shadows quickly
thickened. I flicked my horse's reins, descended into a
hollow, crossed a dried-up stream overgrown with
willow bushes, and climbed uphill into a forest. The
winding road ahead of me ran among thick hazel
bushes, already shrouded in darkness, and it was hard
to go forward. The droshky jolted over the tough roots

of hundred-year-old oaks and limes as it ran along the deep ruts left by cartwheels, and my horse stumbled. A sudden violent gust of wind rushed hissing through the treetops overhead, and heavy raindrops rattled and pattered over the leaves. Lightning flashed, and the storm broke. The rain fell in sheets. I carried on at a walk, but soon had to stop altogether, for my horse was sinking into the mud, and I couldn't see a thing. I sheltered as best I could next to a spreading bush. Crouching down on my seat and covering my face, I waited patiently for the storm to pass. Suddenly, by a flash of lightning, I thought I saw a tall figure, and as I continued to stare that way, the figure seemed to rise out of the ground beside my droshky.

'Who are you?' came a resonant voice.

'Who are you yourself?'

'I'm the forester here.'

I told him my name.

'Oh, I know you! On your way home?'

'Yes. But you can see the storm . . .'

'Yes, there's a storm,' replied the voice.

A flash of white lightning lit up the forester from head to foot, and a sharp cracking thunderclap followed an instant later. The rain poured down harder than ever.

'This won't be over any time soon,' the forester said.

'What can one do!'

'I'd better take you to my hut,' he said shortly.

'That's kind of you.'

'Stay where you are, then.'

He went to my horse's head and pulled on her bridle. We moved off. I held on to the upholstered seat of the droshky, which was rocking like a boat on the high seas, and called my dog. My poor mare was squelching through the mud, slithering and stumbling along, while the forester swayed this way and that like a ghost in front of the shafts. We drove along for quite a while, but eventually my guide stopped. 'Here we are, mister, we've arrived,' he said in a low voice. A wicket gate creaked, and several puppies started barking in chorus. I looked up; in the glare of a lightning flash I glimpsed a little hut in the middle of a wide yard enclosed by a wattle fence. A dim light showed in a window. The forester led my horse up to the entrance and knocked. 'Coming! Coming!' came a piping little voice, followed by the patter of bare feet. The bolt scraped open, and a girl of twelve in a smock tied with a strip of cloth appeared in the doorway, holding a lantern.

'Light the gentleman in,' he told her, and added 'I'll put your droshky under cover.'

The girl glanced at me and went back in. I followed her.

The forester's hut consisted of a single smoky room, low-pitched and empty. There were no bunks and no partition. A ragged sheepskin hung on the wall. I saw a single-barrelled shotgun lying on a bench, a heap of rags in a corner, and two big pots standing by the fire. A taper was burning on the table, flaring up dismally and fading out. A cradle hung in the middle of the hut, suspended on the end of a long pole. The girl blew out her lantern, sat down on the tiny bench and began rocking the cradle with her right hand while attending to the taper with her left. I looked around with a sinking heart. A peasant's hut at night is not a cheerful place. The baby in the cradle was breathing hard and rapidly.

'Are you all on your own here?' I asked the girl.

'Yes,' she replied, so softly that I could barely hear her.

'Are you the forester's daughter?'

'That's right,' she whispered.

The door creaked and the forester strode in, head bowed. He picked up the lantern from the floor, brought it to the table and lit it.

'Not used to tapers, I guess?' he said, tossing back his curly hair.

I looked at him. Rarely had I seen such a fine-look-ing young man. He was tall, broad-shouldered, and splendidly built. His powerful muscles bulged under his damp canvas shirt. His stern, manly face was half hidden behind a curly black beard; small brown eyes looked boldly out under a pair of thick eyebrows that met over his nose. He stood facing me, resting his hands lightly on his hips.

I thanked him for taking me in, and asked his name.

*'Foma,' he said. 'They call me Biryuk.'

'Ah, you're Biryuk, are you?'

I looked at him again, with redoubled curiosity. I had often heard tales about Biryuk the forester, from my man Yermolay and others. Apparently all the peasants around dreaded him worse than fire. Never, they said, had the world known such a master of his trade. 'He won't let you take so much as a handful of brushwood; he'll come down on you like snow off a roof, any time of day, even at midnight, and don't even think of standing up to him—he's strong, and nimble as the devil himself . . . And there's no getting round him, not with vodka, nor money either, nothing'll tempt him. Time and again our good folk have tried to get rid of him, but there's no chance, he's too much for them.'

* In Orel province, 'Biryuk' is the name given to a morose, solitary man. [Author's note]

That was what the local peasants said about him.

'So you're Biryuk,' I repeated. 'I've heard about you, my man. They say you never let anybody off.'

'I do my duty,' he replied sullenly. 'It's not right to eat the master's bread for nothing.'

He took an axe out of his belt, sat down on the floor and began splitting off a wooden taper.

'Haven't you got a woman?' I asked.

'No,' he said, brandishing his axe.

'Died, I suppose?'

'No . . . yes . . . dead,' he said and turned away.

I said nothing. He raised his head and looked at me.

'Ran off with a passing tradesman,' he said with a bitter smile. The girl hung her head. The baby woke and started crying, and the girl went over to the cradle. 'Here, give him this,' said Biryuk, thrusting a dirty feeding horn into her hand. 'Left him, too,' he went on in an undertone, pointing to the baby. He got up and went over to the door, stood there and turned round.

'You won't want to eat any of our bread, I dare say, mister,' he began. 'But apart from bread, that's all I—'

'I'm not hungry.'

'Just as you like. I'd light the samovar for you, but I've no tea . . . I'll take a look at your horse.'

He went out and banged the door. I looked about me again. The hut seemed more dismal than ever.

The bitter smell of stale smoke was making breathing difficult. The girl never moved from her seat nor raised her eyes; now and then she gave the cradle a push, and timidly pulled the top of her shift up over her shoulder. Her bare feet hung down, motionless.

'What's your name?' I asked.

'Ulita,' she replied, bowing her sad little head even lower.

The forester came back in and seated himself on the bench.

'The storm's passing,' he remarked after a short silence. 'I'll see you out of the wood if you want.'

I stood up. Biryuk picked up his gun and checked the pan.

'What's that for?'

'They're up to no good, in the woods . . . They're chopping a tree down at Mare's Rise,' he added in response to my look of enquiry.

'You mean you can hear it from here?'

'From outside.'

We went out together. The rain had stopped. Heavy masses of storm clouds were still crowding the horizon, with long jagged lightnings flashing now and then, but overhead there were patches of deep-blue night sky, with stars twinkling through the swiftly scudding clouds. Through the darkness I began to make out the outlines of trees, drenched with rain and blowing in the wind. We stood and listened. The forester took off his cap and lowered his head. 'There . . . there it is,' he said suddenly, raising his arm. 'What a night to choose.'

I could hear nothing but the leaves rustling. Biryuk led my horse out. 'But if we go like this,' he reflected, 'I'll probably miss him.'

'I'll come with you on foot . . . shall I?'

'All right,' he said, and backed my horse under cover again. 'We'll catch him in no time, and then I'll see you out of the wood. Let's go.'

We set off, Biryuk in front and I following him. God knows how he found the way, but he only stopped occasionally, and that was to listen to the sound of the axe.

'There it is,' he muttered through clenched teeth. 'Hear it? Do you?'

'But where is it?'

Biryuk shrugged. We climbed down into a ravine, the wind eased off for a moment, and now I could clearly hear the measured blows. Biryuk looked at me and shook his head. On we went, through wet ferns and nettles. Then we heard a long, deep crashing sound.

'It's down . . .' muttered Biryuk.

Meanwhile the sky was growing clearer and clearer; a faint light was showing in the forest. Finally we clambered out of the ravine. 'Wait here,' the forester whispered, bending forward and holding his gun above his head. He vanished into the bushes. I listened as hard as I could; over the constant howl of the wind, I thought I could hear faint sounds not far away. An axe cautiously tapping against small branches, a wheel creaking, a horse snorting . . .

'Where are you off to? Stop there!' thundered Biryuk's iron voice. Another voice gave a pitiful cry, like a trapped hare . . . A fight was starting. 'No, you don't! No, you don't,' panted Biryuk, 'you're not getting away from me . . .'

I rushed towards the noise, tripping up at every step; when I reached the battleground, I found the felled tree lying on the ground, and the forester kneeling beside it, holding the thief down and tying his hands behind his back with his belt. I came up to them. Biryuk stood up and raised the thief onto his feet. I saw a peasant covered in sodden rags, with a long unkempt beard; his scruffy little horse, half covered with a stiff cloth, was standing nearby, harnessed to a log cart. The forester wasn't saying a word; the peasant, too, was standing silently by, shaking his head.

'Let him go,' I whispered in Biryuk's ear. 'I'll pay for the tree.'

Biryuk said nothing. He took the horse by the mane in his left hand, and held on to the thief by the belt with his right.

'Turn around, you scum,' he said grimly.

'Take the little axe,' mumbled the peasant.

'No point letting that go, that's true,' said the forester, picking up the axe. We set off. I followed the other two . . . The rain was starting to patter down again, and soon it was pouring in sheets. We had trouble getting back to the hut. Biryuk left the confiscated horse in the middle of the yard, led the peasant indoors, loosened the knot on his belt and sat him in a corner. The girl, who had fallen asleep by the fire, jumped to her feet and stared at us in dumb terror. I sat down on the bench.

'Look at it pouring down,' remarked the forester. 'You'll have to wait a bit. Would you like to lie down?'

'No, thanks.'

'I'd have locked him in the storeroom, on account of you, sir,' he went on, indicating the peasant; 'but you see, the bolt on the door—'

'Let him stay here, don't touch him,' I interrupted.

The peasant cast me a furtive glance. I silently promised myself to set the poor wretch free, no matter what. He was sitting motionless on the bench; by the light of the lantern I could see his haggard, wrinkled face, his heavy, sandy-coloured eyebrows, restless eyes, skinny limbs . . . The girl lay down on the floor at his feet and fell asleep again. Biryuk was sitting by the table, resting his head on his hands. A cricket chirped in the corner. The rain rattled on the roof and ran down the windows. None of us spoke.

'Foma Kuzmich,' the peasant suddenly spoke up, in a dull, broken voice. 'Eh, Foma Kuzmich.'

'What?'

'Let me go.'

Biryuk didn't answer.

'Let me go . . . We were starving . . . let me go.'

'I know you lot,' the forester answered grimly, 'you're all the same, your whole village—one thief after another.'

'Let me go,' the peasant repeated. 'Our bailiff . . . we're ruined, that's what . . . let me go!'

'Ruined indeed! . . . Nobody has to steal.'

'Let me go, Foma Kuzmich . . . Don't destroy me. Your boss, you know him yourself—he'll eat me alive, that's what.'

Biryuk turned away. The peasant was shaking as though he had a high fever, tossing his head about and breathing in broken gasps.

'Let me go,' he repeated in gloomy desperation. 'Let me go, in God's name, let me go! I'll pay, I really will, honest to God. I swear by God, we're starving . . .

the children crying, you know what it's like. Life's hard for us, it is.'

'All the same, you shouldn't go thieving.'

'The little horse,' the peasant said, 'my little horse, at least . . . the only beast we've got . . . let her go!'

'I'm telling you—I can't. I'm under orders myself, I'll be held responsible. I can't be soft on you people.'

'Let me go! We're starving, Foma Kuzmich, starving, and that's the truth . . . Let me go!'

'I know you!'

'Let me go, please!'

'Huh, what's the good of talking to you? Sit still and shut up, or you know what'll happen. Can't you see there's a gentleman here?'

The poor wretch hung his head . . . Biryuk yawned and laid his head on the table. The rain kept on and on. I waited to see what would happen.

Suddenly the peasant stood up. His eyes blazed, the colour came to his cheeks. 'All right then, eat me, go on, and I hope you choke, go on . . .' he began, screwing up his eyes and turning down the corners of his mouth. 'Go on, then, you cursed murderer—drink a Christian's blood, go on, drink it . . .'

The forester turned round.

'Yes, it's you I'm talking to, Asiatic scum, bloodsucker, you!'

'Drunk, are you? Cursing and swearing like that?' the forester demanded in astonishment. 'Are you out of your mind?'

'Drunk, is it? On your money? You cursed murderer, you brute, brute, brute!'

'Ah you . . . wait till I get you!'

'What do I care? It's all the same—I'm done for! What'll I do without my horse? Bang me on the head, there's no difference; die of hunger, or die here and now, it's all the same. Do for the lot of us, my wife, my children, kill them all . . . But just you wait, we'll get you in the end!'

Biryuk rose to his feet.

'Kill me, kill me,' the peasant snarled savagely, 'kill me, go on, here I am, kill me . . .' (The girl jumped quickly up from the floor and stared at him.) 'Kill me, kill me!'

'Shut up!' roared the forester, taking two steps forward.

'Stop! That'll do, Foma!' I cried. 'Let him be! Leave him alone.'

'I won't shut up!' the poor wretch went on. 'It's all the same to me if you kill me. You murderer, you animal, you merciless brute . . . But just you wait, you won't be strutting round for long! They'll wring your neck for you, you wait!'

Biryuk grabbed him by the shoulder . . . I rushed over to protect the poor peasant . . .

'Hands off, master!' the forester shouted at me.

I wasn't scared by his threat, and had already flung out my arm; but to my utter amazement, he wrenched the belt off the peasant's elbows in a single jerk, seized him by the scruff of the neck, tugged his cap down over his eyes, pulled open the door and shoved him outside.

'Go to hell, and take your horse with you!' he shouted after him. 'But you watch out, don't let me ever catch you again!'

He came back into the hut and started rummaging in a corner.

'Well, Biryuk,' I eventually said, 'you've surprised me. You're a good fellow, I see.'

'Enough of that, sir,' he interrupted me in vexed tones, 'and please don't tell anyone. Anyway, I'd better take you back,' he added; 'there's no point waiting for this rain to stop . . .'

Outside in the yard we heard the peasant's cart rumbling away.

'So he's gone!' muttered Biryuk. 'But next time . . .!'

Half an hour later he saw me off at the edge of the wood.

THE RATTLING!

'Got something to tell you,' said Yermolay, coming into my hut, where I'd finished eating and was lying on my camp bed to rest after a pretty successful but tiring day out shooting grouse. It was the middle of July, during a tremendous heat-wave. 'Got something to tell you—we're out of shot.'

I jumped up off the bed.

'Out of shot! How on earth? When we brought something like thirty pounds of it with us from the village! A whole bag of it!'

'That's right, and a big bag too. Should have lasted us a couple of weeks. But who knows—the bag might have got a hole in it . . . Anyway, that's how it is, there's no shot . . . perhaps enough for ten more charges.'

'So what'll we do now? We're just getting to the best spots—we were promised six coveys tomorrow . . .'

'Send me off to Tula—it's not far, just forty-five versts. I'll ride there and back like the wind and bring back the shot, forty pounds of it if you want.'

'When'll you go?'

'Right now if you like. Why wait? Only there's one thing—we'll have to hire horses.'

'Whatever for? What about our own?'

'Can't use our own. The shaft horse has gone lame. Quite badly.'

'When did that happen?'

'Just the other day. The driver took him to be shod. And they did a shoddy job of it too. Must have been a clumsy blacksmith. Now the horse can't even put his hoof down. It's his front hoof—he's holding it off the ground, like a dog.'

'So—have they got the shoe off, at least?'

'No, they haven't, but that's what needs doing. The nail must have gone right into the flesh.'

I sent for the driver. Yermolay turned out to be right: the shaft horse was holding his hoof off the ground. I gave orders at once for the animal to be unshod and stood on damp clay.

'So will you hire some horses to go to Tula?' Yermolay persisted.

'How can we get hold of any horses out here in the sticks?' I exclaimed peevishly. The village we were staying in was a desolate place in the back of beyond, where all the villagers looked like paupers. We had trouble finding a single decent-sized hut, and even that one had no chimney.

'We'll get some,' replied Yermolay, as impassive as ever. 'What you said about this village was right enough; but there used to be one peasant living here, a clever man, and rich too, and he had nine horses. Well, he's dead now, but his eldest son has taken it all on. He's as thick as they come, but he hasn't managed to run through all his father's money yet. We'll get hold of some horses from him. Say the word and I'll bring him over here. It seems his brothers are quite smart—though he's in charge all the same.'

'Why's that?'

'Just because. He's the eldest, so the younger ones have to jump to it and do as he says.' Yermolay added something juicy and unprintable about younger broth-ers in general. 'I'll get him over here. He's a bit simple. You'll have no trouble agreeing terms with him.'

While Yermolay was on his way to get this 'simple' peasant, it occurred to me that I had better go to Tula myself. Firstly because I knew from experience not to rely on Yermolay; once I had sent him to town for some provisions, and he had promised to get every-thing I wanted in a single day—after which he didn't come back for a week, drank all my money away, and finally turned up on foot, having set out in a racing droshky. And secondly, I knew a horse dealer in Tula who could sell me a horse to replace my lame shaft horse.

'That settles it!' I thought. 'I'll go myself; and I can sleep on the way—it's a comfortable carriage.'

*

'I've brought him!' cried Yermolay a quarter of an hour later, rushing into the hut. Behind him came a tall, tow-headed peasant wearing a white shirt, dark-blue trousers and bast shoes. He had short-sighted eyes, a sandy-coloured goatee beard, a big bulbous nose and a mouth that hung open. True enough, he looked like a simpleton.

'Here you are,' announced Yermolay: 'He's got the horses, and he's agreeable.'

'That's to say, I mean, I . . .' began the peasant in a hoarse, halting voice, shaking his head with its wispy hair and fingering the band of the cap he held in his hands, 'I . . . that's to say . . .'

'What's your name?' I asked.

He looked down and seemed to be deep in thought.

'My name, you mean?'

'Yes, what's your name?'

'Well, my name—that'll be Filofey.'

'Well now, friend Filofey, I'm told you've got horses. Bring along a team of three, we'll harness them up to my carriage—it's a light one—and you'll drive me over to Tula. It's a moonlit night, there's plenty of light, and the air will be cool. What's the road like?'

'The road? The road's all right. It'll be twenty versts to the main road, not more. There's one place that's . . . tricky; otherwise it's all right.'

'What's the place that's tricky?'

'There's a little river to ford.'

'Why, are you going to Tula yourself?' enquired Yermolay.

'Yes.'

'Well!' said my faithful retainer, tossing his head. 'We-e-ell!' he repeated, spat and left the room.

Evidently the drive to Tula no longer held any attraction for him. It had turned into a dull and point-less chore.

'Do you know the road well?' I asked Filofey.

''Course I do! Only I, begging your pardon, mister, I can't go . . . all of a sudden, like . . .'

It turned out that when Yermolay was negotiating with Filofey, he had told him that he'd definitely be paid . . . and left it at that! And Filofey, though Yermolay described him as an idiot, wasn't satisfied. He demanded fifty roubles in banknotes from me—a huge sum. I offered him ten, a low one. And we started haggling; Filofey dug his heels in at first, but then began to come down, very slowly. When Yermolay looked into the room for a moment, he assured me that 'that idiot' ('Ain't he fond of that word!' Filofey remarked under his breath) 'that idiot has no idea of the value of money'. He reminded me in passing that some twenty years ago, my mother had set up a post-ing inn at a perfect spot where two high roads crossed, and the business had failed dismally because the old house serf who was put in charge had no idea of the value of money. He thought that the more coins there were, the better, so he would pay out a silver quarter rouble in change for half a dozen coppers, though cursing furiously all the while.

'Huh, Filofey—you're a right Filofey!' Yermolay exclaimed at last, and went out, angrily slamming the door.

Filofey did not answer, seeming to accept that being called Filofey really wasn't very clever of him and that it was quite fair to hold it against him, though it was really the priest's fault—obviously the man hadn't been properly paid for the baptism.

We finally agreed on twenty roubles. He set off to get the horses, and an hour later returned with no fewer than five for me to choose from. They were decent horses, though their manes and tails were tangled and their bellies swollen and stretched tight as drums. Filofey was accompanied by two brothers, who looked nothing like him. Small, dark-eyed, with sharp noses, they really did look like 'smart lads'. They talked a lot and very fast—'yacking away', as Filofey put it—but they deferred to their elder brother.

They wheeled my carriage out from under its awning and spent an hour and a half getting it and the horses ready, first letting out the harness straps and then pulling them far too tight . . . Both brothers were very keen to harness up 'the roan one' because 'him'll get down the hills better', but Filofey decided on a horse he called 'Shaggy', so Shaggy it was that was put between the shafts.

They loaded the carriage up with hay, and put the lame shaft horse's collar under the seat in case it needed to be used on a new horse, if we bought one in Tula. Filofey had managed to run home and come back wearing his father's long white overcoat, a tall cap and tarred boots, and now he climbed majestically onto the box. I got into the carriage and looked at my watch: ten fifteen. Yermolay didn't even say goodbye to me, but just set about beating his dog Valetka. Filofey flicked the reins and called out 'Gee up, my little ones!' in a faint, thin voice. His brothers leapt up to tap the two

trace horses on the belly, and the carriage moved off.
As it turned out of the gates into the road, Shaggy tried
to make off homewards, but Filofey dissuaded him with
a few lashes of his whip, and in a moment we had left
the village behind and were bowling along a smooth
road through a dense avenue of bushy hazels.

It was a blissfully quiet night, perfect for travelling.
Sometimes the wind rustled through the bushes and
set the branches moving; then it would die away
completely. Here and there, silvery clouds hung
motionless in the sky. The moon was high overhead,
casting a brilliant light over the landscape. I stretched
out on the hay and was about to fall asleep . . . until I
gave a start as I remembered the 'tricky' place.

'Say, Filofey—how far to the ford?'

'The ford? It'll be about eight versts.'

'Eight versts,' I thought. 'We won't be there for an
hour or more. I could take a little nap.'

'Filofey, do you know the road well?' I asked again.

'Why shouldn't I know it? It's not my first time . . .'

He went on, but I didn't hear him. I was asleep.

*

I woke after exactly an hour—not because I'd made
up my mind to do it (though that often happens). I was
woken by a strange sound, a sort of quiet lapping and
gurgling, right by my ear. I raised my head . . .

What on earth had happened? I was lying in the carriage as before, but all around it, and not more than a foot below the sides, was an expanse of smooth water, gleaming in the moonlight, shimmering and trembling with tiny ripples. Up in front, sitting like a statue on the box, with his head drooping and his back bowed, was Filofey; and ahead of him, rising up out of the rolling waters, was the arch of the yoke and the backs and heads of our horses. It was all so still and noiseless, as if we were in an enchanted kingdom, or in a dream, a magical dream ... What could have happened? I glanced back under the carriage hood ... Why, we were right in the middle of the river! The bank was all of thirty paces behind us!

'Filofey!' I cried out.

'Yes, what is it?'

'What do you mean, what is it? For heaven's sake! Where have we got to?'

'In the river.'

'Yes, I can see we're in the river. Another minute and we'll be underwater. Is this how you cross a ford? Eh? You're fast asleep, Filofey! Answer me!'

'I've gone a bit wrong,' said my driver. 'I went too far over to one side. Now we've got to wait.'

'What do you mean, got to wait? What on earth are we waiting for?'

'Just to let Shaggy take a look around. When he sets off, that's the way we've got to go.'

I raised myself up on the hay. The shaft horse's head was hanging motionless over the water. All you could see in the bright moonlight was one of his ears giving a tiny twitch backwards and forwards.

'But he's asleep himself, your Shaggy!'

'No he's not,' replied Filofey. 'He's just sniffing the water now.' And once again silence descended, save for the faint lapping of the water. I fell into a daze myself.

The moonlight, and the night, and the river—and us in the middle of it . . .

'What's that croaking sound?' I asked.

'That? That's ducklings in the rushes . . . unless it's snakes.'

All of a sudden the shaft horse shook his head and pricked up his ears; then he gave a snort, and started moving.

'Go-go-go-go-o-o!' Filofey suddenly yelled at the top of his voice, rising up on the box and waving his whip in the air. The carriage gave a jolt and lurched forward across the current—and carried on, bumping and swaying . . . At first it looked as if we were going down, sinking deeper into the water; but after two or three jolts and plunges the expanse of water around us seemed to have suddenly fallen away . . . Down and down it went, as the carriage rose out of it—and now the wheels came into view, and the horses' tails; and at last, scattering powerful great splashes like sheaves of diamond drops—no, not diamond, sapphire drops— glittering on all sides of us in the pale light of the moon—the horses pulled gamely together, heaved out onto the sandy riverbank, and then set off uphill, with their gleaming wet legs flashing in turn, one after the other.

'What's Filofey going to say now?' I wondered. 'Will it be "I was right all along!"—or something like that?' But he said nothing. And so I, too, felt it unnecessary to scold him for his carelessness. I stretched out on the hay and tried to get to sleep again.

But I couldn't sleep—not because I hadn't tired myself out hunting today, nor because my recent alarm had chased sleep away, but because we were now passing through some very beautiful country. Broad, rolling, grassy flood plains, many little meadows, ponds and streams; creeks choked with tangles of osiers—the real Russian countryside, that we Russians love so well—like the lands that our heroes traversed in ancient times, on their way to shoot white swans or grey ducks. Our track wound along in a yellowish ribbon, our horses were running effortlessly on, and I was so lost in admiration that I could not shut my eyes. It was all flowing past me so gently and evenly, under the friendly moon above. Even Filofey felt the spell.

'These meadows, they're called Saint Yegor's,' he told me. 'And beyond them, those'll be Grand Duke's; there's no meadows like these in all Russia . . . Lovely, they are!' The shaft horse snorted and shook itself. 'Lord bless you!' murmured Filofey solemnly under his breath. 'Lovely!' he repeated, with a deep sigh followed by a series of grunts. 'Soon the haymaking'll begin, and the loads of hay they'll cut around here, you wouldn't believe! And them creeks, they're full of fish, too. The bream—wonderful!' he added in a lilting voice. 'What I mean—you just wish you'd never have to die!'

Suddenly he raised an arm.

'Hey! Look over there! On that lake! Isn't that a heron standing there? Catching fish, even at night? Oh my, no, that's a branch, not a heron at all. Put my foot in it, didn't I? That moon makes a fool of you.'

We drove on and on . . . And here the meadows came to an end, and little thickets appeared, and ploughed fields; a hamlet to one side of us showed us two or three winking lights . . . only five versts more till the main road. I fell asleep.

Once again I didn't wake of my own accord. This time it was Filofey's voice that roused me.

'Mister! Hey, mister!'

I sat up. The carriage had stopped on a patch of flat ground right in the middle of the main road. Filofey had turned round from the box to face me, his eyes wide open (I was surprised to see what very large eyes he had), and said in an impressive, mysterious whisper:

'That rattling! . . . The rattling!'

'What do you mean?'

'I said—the rattling! Bend your head down and listen. Can you hear it?'

I leaned my head out of the carriage, held my breath—and sure enough, somewhere far, far behind us I could hear a soft intermittent rattling sound, like rolling wheels.

'Hear it?' repeated Filofey.

'Well, yes,' I said. 'There's some carriage coming along.'

'But can't you hear . . . Sssshh! There—jingling bells . . . and whistling . . . Hear it? Take off your cap, you'll hear better.'

I didn't take off my cap, but I listened hard.

'Well, yes . . . perhaps. But so what?'

Filofey turned back to face the horses.

'That's a cart coming . . . empty, with iron rims on its wheels,' he said, gathering up the reins. 'That's bad people coming, mister. They get up to all sorts of tricks hereabouts, round Tula. A load of mischief.'

'What rubbish! What makes you so sure it's got to be bad people?'

'I know what I'm saying. Jingling bells . . . and an empty cart . . . Who else could it be?'

'Well . . . is it far to Tula?'

'It'll be another fifteen versts. And there's no houses round here.'

'Well then, get on as quick as you can, best not hang about.'

Filofey waved his whip, and the carriage rolled on again.

*

I didn't believe Filofey, but I couldn't get back to sleep. Supposing he was right, after all? An ominous feeling stirred inside me. I sat up in the carriage—till then I had been lying down—and looked out first to one side and then the other. A light mist had blown in while I slept—not over the ground but over the sky. It hung there, high overhead, with the moon a pale smudge behind it, as though seen through smoke. Everything had grown darker and more indistinct, though nearer the ground the visibility was better. The countryside around was flat and dreary—fields, and more fields, the odd shrub here and there, gullies and more fields, and patches of mist, and an occasional clump of weeds. A desolate, lifeless scene! Not even a quail calling!

We had been driving about half an hour. Filofey kept waving his whip and clicking his tongue, but neither of us said a word. Now we were climbing uphill . . . Filofey stopped the team and instantly said:

'Rattling, mister! That rattling!'

I leaned out of the carriage again—but I could have stayed under the awning, for I could hear it very clearly now, though it was still a long way off. There was the sound of the cartwheels, and men whistling, and the jingle of little bells, and the horses' very hoof beats. I even imagined I could hear singing and laughter. The wind, it was true, was blowing from that direction, but there was no doubt that these unknown travellers had gained a whole verst on us, if not two.

Filofey and I glanced at each other. Then he just shifted his hat forward over his forehead, leaned over the reins and at once set to whipping up the horses. They galloped ahead, but they couldn't gallop for long, and soon slowed to a trot again. Filofey went on whipping them. We had to get away!

I had no idea why I now suddenly became convinced that Filofey, whose fears I had not shared before, was right, and that there really were bad people

following behind . . . There was nothing new to hear—
the same jingling bells, the same rattling of the empty
cart, the same whistling and jumble of noises . . . but
now I had no doubt. Filofey couldn't be wrong!

Another twenty minutes or so went by . . . And by
the end of those twenty minutes, we could clearly
hear, over the rattling and rumbling of our own
carriage, the rattling and rumbling of the other . . .

'Pull up, Filofey!' I said. 'It's no use—it won't make
any difference now.'

Filofey uttered a timid 'Whoa there!' and the horses
drew up at once, as if relieved to be able to rest.

Heavens above! Those bells were jangling right
behind us, the cart rattling and bumping over the
road, and the people whistling, shouting and singing,
and their horses snorting and stamping on the
ground . . .

They had caught us up!

'A-a-all up with us,' muttered Filofey slowly under
his breath. He gave a half-hearted click of his tongue
to get the horses going again; but at that very instant
there was a sudden rushing, roaring, tearing noise, and
a huge wide cart drawn by three wiry horses swerved
sharply round our carriage, swept ahead and immediately slowed to a walk, blocking the road in front.

'A regular bandits' trick,' whispered Filofey.

I must confess that I felt a chill at my heart . . . I stared hard into the half-darkness, where the moonlight was obscured by mist. Half sitting, half sprawling in the cart ahead of us were some six men in shirts and open rough coats, two of them bareheaded; the men's big booted legs were dangling over the cart sides, their arms rising and falling aimlessly, their bodies swaying . . . No doubt about it, these people were all drunk. Some were bellowing meaningless words at the tops of their voices, one was giving shrill, piercing whistles, another was cursing and swearing. A giant in a sheepskin jacket was sitting in the driver's seat holding the reins. They drove on at a walking pace, seemingly taking no notice of us.

What could we do? We followed on behind, also at a walk . . . willy-nilly. And so we advanced a few hundred yards. The waiting was torture . . . Should we run away? Or make a stand? . . . But what chance did we have? There were six of them, and I didn't even have a stick. Should we turn the carriage back? But they'd catch up with us in no time. I remembered a line from Zhukovsky's poem (where he describes the murder of Field Marshal Kamensky):

. . . *The highwayman's foul axe* . . .

Or else—throttled with a filthy rope . . . tossed into a ditch . . . and you'll struggle and choke there like a rabbit in a snare . . .

No, it wasn't looking good!

They carried on at a walking pace, taking no notice of us.

'Filofey,' I whispered, 'try driving to the right a bit, see if you can get past.'

Filofey tried, and bore to the right—but the others bore to the right too, and there was no way we could overtake.

Then he had another try, and bore to the left . . . but once again they stopped him getting past . . . They even laughed. So they weren't going to let us by.

'Robbers sure enough,' Filofey whispered over his shoulder.

'So what are they waiting for?' I whispered back.

'Over ahead, there's a hollow, and a bridge over a stream . . . That's where they'll get us! That's what they always do . . . by a bridge. We're well and truly done for, mister!' he sighed. 'They'll never let us go alive—the main thing for them is—wrap it all up and no one the wiser! One thing I'm sorry about, mister: this is the end of my three horses, and my brothers'll never get them.'

I almost wondered at Filofey, fretting about his horses at a moment like this; but I must confess I didn't have much thought to spare for him either . . . 'Will they really kill us?' I wondered over and over again. 'What for? When I'll give them all I've got anyway?'

The bridge was getting closer and closer, clearer and clearer ahead of us . . .

Suddenly we heard loud whoops, their three horses reared up, raced forward, and stopped short when they reached the bridge, standing stock still just off the road. My heart sank.

'Oh, Filofey, brother,' I said, 'you and I are going to our deaths. Forgive me for bringing you to such a sorry end.'

'No fault of yours, mister! There's no escaping our fate. Well now, Shaggy, you faithful little horse of mine,' he went on, talking to the shaft horse, 'get along now! Do one last thing for me! What does it matter now? . . . Lord give us your blessing!'

And he drove his three horses on at a trot.

We were nearing the bridge now, and that ominous, motionless cart . . . And all those men had fallen silent, as if on purpose. Not a sound! Just the way a pike, or a hawk, or any beast of prey, holds itself still when their quarry draws near. Here we were, level with the cart . . . and suddenly the giant in the sheepskin jacket leapt down and made straight for us!

He didn't say a word to Filofey, who instinctively pulled back on the reins. Our carriage stopped.

The giant placed both hands on our doors, leaned his unkempt head forward, bared his teeth in a grin, and spoke in a quiet, unhurried voice, with a drawl like a factory hand:

'Your Honour, sir, we're on our way home from a fine feast, a wedding; we've just married off a young man of ours, and seen him put to bed. All our lads are brave young daredevils, and there's been a great deal drunk, and now we've nothing to clear our heads with. So wouldn't Your Honour be so good and gracious as to spare us a little money, just a trifle, to buy our lads a half-bottle each? We'd remember Your Honour with it, and drink your health. But if you can't help us, well—don't hold it against us!'

'What's all this?' I wondered. 'Is he taunting us? Mocking us?'

The giant still stood there, with his head bowed. At that very moment the moon emerged from the mist and lit up his face. There was a grin on that face—on his lips, and in his eyes too. But there was no hint of a threat . . . it was just a very alert and expectant face . . . and his teeth were so big and so white . . .

'My pleasure . . . here you are . . .' I said hurriedly, pulling my purse out of my pocket and picking out two silver roubles—silver coins were still circulating in Russia back then. 'Here, will this do?'

'Much obliged!' barked the giant in a soldierly voice, while his thick fingers whisked the money away—not the whole purse, just those two roubles. 'Much obliged!' He tossed back his hair and ran to the cart.

'Hey, boys!' he cried, 'His Honour this traveller here has spared us two silver roubles!' The rest of them burst into loud guffaws. The giant clambered back onto his seat . . .

'Look after yourselves!'

And they were gone! The horses dashed off, the cart rumbled uphill—we glimpsed it once more on a dark patch of ground on the skyline; then it vanished over the horizon and was seen no more.

And the rattling, and shouting, and the jingling bells, all faded away too . . .

A deathly silence descended.

*

Filofey and I took some time to come to ourselves.

'Crazy joker that you are!' he said finally. Then he took off his hat and began crossing himself. 'A joker as ever was,' he added, turning to me with a beaming face. 'Well, he must be a good man, for sure. Go-go-go, my little ones! Round you go! You'll live! We'll all live!

And it was him that wouldn't let us past, he was their driver. What a crazy joker! Go-go-go-go-o-o-o! God be with us!'

I said nothing; but I was light at heart. 'We'll live!' I said to myself, and stretched out on the hay. 'We got off lightly!'

I even felt a bit guilty at having recalled that line of Zhukovsky's.

Suddenly something struck me.

'Filofey!'

'What is it?'

'Are you married?'

'Yes.'

'Got any children?'

'Yes, children too.'

'How was it you didn't think of them? You were sorry about the horses—but what about your wife and children?'

'Why feel sad about them? The robbers weren't going to get them. But I had them in my mind all the time—and I've got them there now. That's how it was.' Filofey paused. 'Perhaps . . . perhaps the Lord God had mercy on us two because of them.'

'But if they weren't robbers after all?'

'Who knows? Can you see into someone else's soul? You know the proverb—another's soul is a dark place.

But it's always best to remember God. No . . . I always think of my family . . . Gee up, my little ones, and God be with us!'

It was almost dawn as we drew near to Tula. I was lying in a doze, half asleep . . .

'Hey, mister,' said Filofey all of a sudden. 'Look—there they are, by the inn. That's their cart.'

I looked up. And sure enough, that was them—their cart, and their horses. And suddenly our friend the giant in the sheepskin jacket appeared in the doorway.

'Your Honour!' he called out, waving his cap. 'We're drinking up your money! Well, driver,' he added, jerking his head at Filofey, 'I bet you got a fright back there, eh?'

'What a joker,' remarked Filofey, after driving on fifty yards or so.

We finally reached Tula, where I bought some shot, and some tea and vodka while I was about it, and even a horse from the dealer. At noon we set off on our way back. When we passed the spot where we had first heard the sound of the cart's rattling wheels, Filofey (who'd had a few drinks at Tula, and now turned out to be a very chatty fellow—he'd already told me a whole lot of tall stories) suddenly burst out laughing.

'Remember, mister, how I kept telling you—the rattling, the rattling . . .!'

He made a backhanded gesture . . . He seemed to find that word very funny.

That evening we arrived back at his village.

I told Yermolay what had happened to us. Being sober at the time, he expressed no concern for us, but just gave a snigger—of approval or disapproval, I couldn't say, and I'm sure he couldn't either. But two days later he was delighted to inform me that on that very night when Filofey and I were driving to Tula, a certain merchant had been robbed and murdered on the same road. At first I didn't believe the story, but later I had to, because the police captain sent to investigate the crime confirmed it. So, could that have been the 'wedding' our brave fellows had attended? And could the merchant have been that 'young man of ours' whom they had seen 'put to bed', as the joking giant expressed it? I stayed on another five days in Filofey's village, and whenever I met him, I would say 'Hey! hear that rattling?'

'What a joker!' he'd answer every time, and roar with laughter.

THE DISTRICT DOCTOR

O NE DAY IN autumn I was on my way back from a distant hunting expedition when I caught a feverish cold. Luckily I was staying at an inn in the district town when I fell ill, so I sent for the local doctor. Half an hour later he was there—a short, slight man with dark hair. He prescribed the usual remedy to induce perspiration, and a mustard plaster, and very deftly slipped my five-rouble note up his sleeve, while looking away with a dry cough. He was just about to set off home again, but somehow we got into conversation and he stayed on. My fever had tired me out, and I foresaw a sleepless night, so I was glad of a chat with a pleasant companion. Tea was served, and my doctor began talking. He was a sensible young man, with a vigorous and amusing turn of speech. Life can be strange: sometimes you live for ages with someone you're friendly with, but never have a sincere, heartfelt talk together; and yet when you meet someone you scarcely know, lo and behold, either you're baring your innermost soul to him, or he's doing the same to you, as though you were in the confessional. I have no idea what I had done to deserve my new friend's trust, but however it was, and for no apparent reason, he started telling me about a rather strange experience he'd had. So let me now pass on his story to you, gentle reader, and I'll do my best to tell it in the doctor's own words.

'You don't happen to know,' he began in a weak, quavering voice (such is the effect of unblended Berezovsky tobacco), 'you don't happen to know Mylov, Pavel Lukich, the local judge? You don't? Well, never mind.' (He cleared his throat and rubbed his eyes.) 'Anyway, look, this is how it happened, how can I put it—I don't want to get it wrong—it was during Lent, just when the snows were melting. So there we were, this judge and I, at his place, playing a hand of Preference. Our judge is a fine fellow, and a keen Preference player. And suddenly . . .' (my doctor friend was fond of that word *suddenly*) 'I was told: "Your man is here asking for you." I asked what he wanted, and they said he had brought a note with him, no doubt from a patient. "Let's have it," I said. And so it was—from a patient . . . Ah, well—you must realize, that's what we live on . . . But here's what it was: a local small landowner, a widowed lady, writing to say that her daughter was dying, and would I please come at once, in the name of God Almighty, and she had sent horses for me. Now, that was all very well, but . . . she lived twenty versts out of town, and it was dark outside, and the roads were dreadful. And the woman herself was poor, I couldn't expect more than two silver roubles, if that, or more likely a roll of linen or a bag of groats. But duty calls, you know, here was someone dying. So I passed my hand over to Kalliopin right away, he's always there, and set off home. And what did I see but a little trap drawn up by the porch, with peasant's horses, fat as butter, with shaggy coats like felt, and the driver sitting there bareheaded out of respect. Well, my friend, I thought, no question about it, your people aren't rolling in money . . . You're smiling, sir, but let me tell you, people like us who aren't well off, we have to take account of everything . . . If a coachman sits there like a prince, and doesn't doff his cap, and he's laughing into his beard at you, and flicking his whip— well then, go for it, hold out for a couple of banknotes! But there wasn't a whiff of that here. Anyway, I said to myself, there's no help for it, duty calls. So I snatched up all the essential medicines and we set off. Believe me, we barely made it through. The road was infernal—streams running across it, and snow, and mud, and gullies full of floodwater, and in one place a dyke had broken through—terrible! Anyway, we got there. So it's a little house with a thatched roof, and lights in the windows—that means they're waiting up for me. And in I go. And a venerable old lady in a cap comes to meet me. "Save her," she begs me, "she's dying." And I tell her, "Please don't worry . . . Where's the patient?" "Would you come this way?" So I look in, and it's a clean room, with a lamp in the corner, and a girl of about twenty lying on the bed unconscious. You could feel the heat coming off her, she's breathing heavily, she's in a high fever. And two other girls are there, her sisters, scared out of their wits, in floods of tears. "Listen," they tell me, "she was perfectly well yesterday, enjoying her food, and this morning she complained of a headache, and by evening she was like this . . ." So I tell them again, "Please don't worry"—we doctors, you know, we have to say that—and I go over to her. I bled her, and ordered a mustard plaster, and prescribed a mixture. And all the while I'm looking at her, looking, you know—honest to God, I'd never in my life seen a face like hers—what a beauty, I mean! I felt so sorry for her, unbearably sorry! She had such sweet features, and those eyes . . . By now she had become easier, thank God; she'd broken into a sweat, and seemed to come to herself; she looked round, and smiled, and passed her hand over her face . . . Her sisters bent over her and asked, "How are you?"—"All right," she says, and turns her face away . . . And when I look, she's fallen asleep. Well, I say, now we have to leave the patient to rest. And we all tiptoed out of the room, only the maid stayed behind, just in case. And in the parlour the samovar was waiting on the table, and a bottle of rum beside it. In our business, you can't get on without that. I was served a glass of tea, and invited to stay the night . . . I accepted—how could I have left, at that hour! The old lady went on sighing. "What is it?" I asked. "She'll live, please don't worry. You'd better get some rest yourself—it's gone one o'clock."—"But you'll get them to wake me if anything happens?"—"Yes, of course." The old lady went out, and the girls went to their own room. A bed had been made up for me in the parlour. I lay down, but I couldn't get to sleep, strangely enough—though I was worn out. I couldn't get my patient out of my head. Eventually I couldn't help myself, and got up. I'll go and see how my patient is getting on, I thought. Her room was next door to the parlour. So I quietly went and opened her door. My heart was pounding. I found the maid fast asleep, with her mouth wide open; she was actually snoring, the brute! The sick girl was lying there facing me, her

arms outspread, poor thing! I stepped closer . . .
Suddenly she opened her eyes and fixed them on
me! . . . "Who is it? Who are you?" I was embarrassed.
"Don't be frightened, young lady," I said. "I'm the
doctor, come to see how you are."—"You're a
doctor?"—"Yes, that's right . . . Your mother sent to
town to fetch me. We've let some blood, and now you
have to get some sleep, and in a day or two, God willing, we'll have you on your feet again."—"Oh yes,
Doctor, please don't let me die . . . please, please
don't!"—"For heaven's sake, what are you thinking
of!" But she's got her fever back again, I thought. I felt
her pulse: yes, I was right, the fever was back. She
looked at me—and suddenly gripped my hand very
hard. "I'll tell you why I don't want to die, I'll tell you,
I'll tell you . . . we're on our own now; but please don't
you tell anyone . . . listen . . ." I bent over her and she
brought her lips right up to my ear—her hair was
touching my neck—I must tell you, my own head was
spinning—and she started whispering something . . . I
couldn't make out a thing . . . she must be delirious, I
thought . . . she whispered on and on, so fast, and it
didn't sound like Russian, and then she finished, and
gave a start, and let her head fall back on the pillow,
and held up a warning finger. "Remember, Doctor,
not a word . . ." Somehow or other I managed to

reassure her, gave her something to drink, woke the maid and went out.'

The doctor helped himself to more snuff, sniffed furiously, and seemed to freeze for an instant.

'Anyway,' he went on, 'next day, unexpectedly for me, my patient was no better. I thought and thought, and suddenly decided to stay there, although I had other patients waiting . . . You know, you can't ignore that sort of thing, or your practice suffers. But for one thing, the sick girl was really in a desperate state, and for another, I have to say, I myself felt strongly drawn to her. And I liked the whole family, too. Although they weren't well off, they were uncommonly cultured people. The father had been a learned man, a writer; he had died poor, but he'd managed to give his children an excellent education, and left a lot of books too. It might have been because I took such trouble over the sick girl, or perhaps for some other reason, but I venture to say that the family came to love me as one of their own . . . Meanwhile the roads had become appalling, all communications cut off, you might say—it was very difficult to get medicines from town, even. The invalid showed no improvement, day after day, day after day . . . Well now . . . that was when . . .' (The doctor fell silent for a while.) 'Honestly, I don't know how to tell you this . . .' (He took another pinch of snuff, coughed and drank a mouthful of tea.) 'I won't beat about the bush. My patient . . . how can I put it . . . well, fell in love with me, didn't she . . . or no, not exactly fell in love . . . though actually . . . honestly, I mean, really . . .' (the doctor blushed and lowered his eyes).

'No,' he went on quickly, 'in love, indeed! I mustn't be giving myself ideas. She was a cultured girl, intelligent and well-read, while I myself had even forgotten my Latin, completely forgotten it. And even my appearance . . .' (he looked down at himself and smiled), 'I don't think I'm anything to boast about. But the good Lord didn't make me a fool either, I know the difference between black and white, I understand a thing or two. For instance, I could see perfectly well that Alexandra Andreyevna, that was her name, felt something for me that wasn't love, it was what you might call a feeling of friendship, or respect—or whatever. Though she herself might have been wrong about that—I mean, just think of her situation . . . Anyway,' the doctor added—he had been uttering all these disjointed sentences in a single breath, evidently highly embarrassed—'I seem to have got a bit carried away . . . you won't be understanding me . . . Listen, I'll tell you everything as it happened.'

He finished his glass of tea and went on in a calmer voice.

'Well then. My patient was getting worse all the time, worse and worse. You're not a doctor, sir—you can't understand what one of us doctors feels like, especially at the start, when it dawns on him that the disease is getting the better of him. What happens to his self-belief? You get so scared—I can't tell you. You feel you've forgotten everything you ever knew, and that the patient doesn't trust you any more, and everyone else is beginning to notice that you haven't a clue, and they don't like to keep you informed about the patient's symptoms, and they look suspiciously at you and whisper to one another . . . oh, it's nasty! And you think, there has to be a medicine for this disease, all I have to do is find it. Mightn't it be this one? You try it out—no, that isn't it! You don't even give the medicine time to work properly . . . you clutch at one thing and then another. You might pick up your compendium of medicines . . . here it is, you think, this is the one! Honestly, I tell you, sometimes you just let the book fall open at random, and leave it to chance . . . And all the time, there's a person dying there, and another doctor could have saved him. So you say there has to be a consultation, I can't take this responsibility on myself alone. What an idiot that makes you look! But you'll get over it in time, it doesn't matter too much. If the person dies, it's not your fault; you stuck to the rules.

But there's a different thing that torments you as well: you see that someone has blind faith in you, and at the same time you feel you can't help. And Alexandra Andreyevna's family had just that kind of blind faith in me. They stopped thinking that their girl was in danger. I myself kept reassuring them that everything was fine, though my heart was in my boots. To make everything even worse, the roads had become so awful that the coachman was away for days on end, getting medicines. And I myself never left my patient's room, I couldn't tear myself away, I kept telling her funny stories, or playing cards with her. And sat by her bedside all night. The old woman was thanking me with tears in her eyes, while I thought to myself, "I don't deserve your thanks." I frankly admit to you— there's no point hiding it any more—I was in love with my patient. And Alexandra Andreyevna had got fond of me too: there were times when she wouldn't let anybody but me into her room. She'd start talking with me, asking me where I had studied, and what my life was like, and what family I had, and whom I visited. And I felt that it wasn't right for her to be talking, but forbidding her, you know, outright, like that—I couldn't do it. Sometimes I'd clutch my head in my hands, and ask myself, what are you up to, you villain? And sometimes she'd take my hand and hold it, and look at me, on and on, and never take her eyes off me, and then turn her head away and sigh, and say "How kind you are!" Her hands were so warm, and she had such big, languid eyes. "Yes," she'd say, "you're a kind, good man, you're not like our neighbours . . . no, you're not like them, not like them . . . Why didn't I know you before?"—"Alexandra Andreyevna," I'd say, "do please keep calm . . . believe me, I've no idea what I've done to deserve . . . only please keep calm, for God's sake, keep calm . . . everything's going to be all right, you're going to get well again." But I have to tell you,' the doctor went on, leaning forward and raising his eyebrows, 'they had very little to do with their neighbours. The ordinary ones weren't up to their level, and they were too proud to mix with the rich ones. I tell you, they were an exceptionally cultured family; and that, you know, flattered me. She wouldn't take her medicine from anyone but me . . . she'd raise herself up, poor little thing, with me helping her, and swallow it, and look at me . . . I felt as if my heart was bursting. And all the time she was getting worse and worse. She's going to die, I thought, she's bound to die. Believe me, I'd rather have lain down in my grave myself. And there were her mother and sisters watching me, looking into my eyes . . . and their confidence draining away. "Well? How is she?"—"Just fine! Don't worry!" Don't worry indeed—when I was almost out of my mind. And one night, there I was, watching by her bedside, all on my own again. And the maid was sitting there too, snoring her head off . . . Well, I couldn't hold it against her, she was exhausted too. Alexandra Andreyevna had been feeling very ill all evening, the fever was draining her. She went on tossing and turning till midnight; at last she seemed to fall asleep, or at least she was lying there not moving. There was a lamp in the corner, burning in front of the holy icon. I'm sitting there, you know, with my eyes down, dozing myself. And suddenly it was as though someone had prodded me in my side, and I turned round . . . Oh my God! Alexandra was staring at me . . . her lips parted, her cheeks burning. "What's wrong?"—"Doctor, I'm going to die, aren't I?"—"God forbid!"—"No, Doctor, no, please don't say I'm going to live . . . Don't say that . . . If you knew . . . Listen to me, for God's sake don't hide anything from me."— Her breathing was coming so fast. "If I know for certain that I have to die, I'll tell you everything—everything!"—"Alexandra Andreyevna, I beg you!"—"Listen, I haven't been asleep at all, I've been watching you for ages . . . for God's sake . . . I trust you, you're a kind man, an honest man, I beg you by all that's holy on earth—tell me the truth! If you knew how important that is for me! . . . Doctor, tell me for God's sake, am I in danger?"—"What can I tell you, Alexandra Andreyevna, for pity's sake?"—"For God's sake, I implore you!"—"I can't hide it from you, Alexandra Andreyevna, yes, you are in danger, but God is merciful . . ."—"So I'm dying, I'm dying . . ." And she seemed to cheer up, her face became so bright, I was scared. "No, don't be afraid, don't be afraid," she says, "I'm not at all afraid of death." All at once she raised herself and leaned on her elbow. "Now . . . well, now I can tell you that I'm grateful to you from the bottom of my heart, you're a kind, good man, and I love you . . ." I stared at her as if I was out of my mind, I felt so terrible, you know . . . "Do you hear—I love you . . ."—"Alexandra Andreyevna, what have I done to deserve that?"—"No, you don't understand! My darling, you don't understand!" And suddenly she held out her arms to me and drew my head to hers and kissed me . . . Believe me, I almost cried out . . . I fell to my knees and hid my face in her pillows. She wasn't saying anything, her fingers were trembling in my hair, I could hear her weeping. I tried to soothe her, to reassure her . . . I really don't know what I said to her. "You'll wake the girl, Alexandra Andreyevna," I said, "thank you . . . believe me . . . keep calm." "No, stop saying that," she kept repeating, "never mind about all of them; what if they do wake up, what if they come in—it doesn't matter, I'm going to die anyway . . . What are you worried about, what are you afraid of, my darling? Lift your head up . . . Or perhaps you don't love me at all, perhaps I've made a mistake . . . if that's how it is, please forgive me."— "Alexandra Andreyevna, what are you saying? I love you, Alexandra Andreyevna!" She looked me full in the eyes, and opened her arms. "Well then, take me in your arms . . ." I'll tell you honestly, I've no idea how I got through that night without going mad. I could feel that my invalid was ruining herself; I could see she wasn't really herself; and I realized that if she hadn't felt she was on the point of death, she'd never have thought of me. But say what you like, it's dreadful to die at twenty-five without ever having loved anyone— that's what was tormenting her, that's why despair had driven her to seize on me—do you understand now? She wouldn't let me out of her arms. "Have pity on me, Alexandra Andreyevna, have pity on yourself too," I said. "What is there to be sorry for? I've got to die anyway!" She never stopped repeating those words. "If I knew that I was going to live, and become a proper young lady again, I'd be ashamed of myself, yes, ashamed . . . but now, so what?"—"But who's told you you're going to die?"—"Oh, no, you can't fool me,

you're no good at lying, just look at yourself."—
"You're going to live, Alexandra Andreyevna, I'm
going to cure you, and we'll ask your mother to give us
her blessing . . . we'll be united, we'll be happy."—
"No, no, you've given me your word, I'm going to
die . . . you promised me . . . you said it . . ." That was
a bitter time for me, bitter for many reasons. And just
think how things sometimes turn out, you think they
don't matter, and yet they hurt. She took it into her
head to ask me my name, I mean my Christian name.
Wasn't it just my luck to be called Trifon. Yes, sir, yes,
Trifon, Trifon Ivanich. Back home everyone just called
me Doctor. But there was nothing for it, I had to tell
her, "Trifon, my lady." She screwed up her eyes, shook
her head and whispered something in French—something unpleasant—and then laughed, unpleasantly
too. And that was how I spent almost the whole of that
night with her. Next morning I left her room, feeling I
had gone mad. I didn't go back to her room till the
afternoon, after tea. Oh my God, my God, I would
never have recognized her—people look better when
they're laid in their grave. I swear to you honestly, I
don't understand, I absolutely don't understand how I
lived through that torture. Three more days, and three
more nights, my sick girl struggled on . . . And what
nights they were! What things she said to me! And on

her last night, just picture it to yourself—I'm sitting by her side and praying to God for just one thing—"Take her to yourself, quickly, and me with her . . ." Suddenly her old mother turns up in the room, unexpectedly. I had told her the day before, the mother I mean, that there wasn't much hope, and it would be a good idea to send for a priest. And the sick girl, as soon as she saw her mother, she says "That's good, that you've come . . . take a look at us, we love each other, we've given each other our word."—"What's she saying, Doctor, what's all that?" I just froze. "Her mind's wandering," I say, "it's her fever . . ."—And she goes, "Stop that, enough of that, you've just been telling me something quite different, and taken a ring from me . . . what are you pretending for, my darling? Mother is kind, she'll forgive us, she'll understand, and I'm dying—there's no reason for me to lie; give me your hand . . ." I jumped up and ran out of the room. The old lady had guessed, naturally.

'Well, I won't wear you out with telling you more. It's hard on me too, I confess, remembering all that. My sick girl died the next day. God rest her soul!' (the doctor added quickly, with a sigh). 'Before she died, she asked all her family to go out and leave me alone with her. "Forgive me," she says, "perhaps I've done you wrong . . . my illness . . . but believe me, I've never loved anybody more than you . . . please don't forget me . . . look after my ring for me . . ." '

The doctor turned away. I took his hand.

'Eh!' he sighed. 'Let's talk about something else. Or would you like a hand of Preference, for small stakes? We doctors, you know, we're not supposed to give way to such sublime sentiments. We're meant to keep our minds on one thing: how to keep the children from squalling and the wife from brawling. I've entered into an honourable marriage, as they call it, since then . . . of course I have . . . A merchant's daughter, with seven thousand roubles. They call her Akulina—it goes perfectly with Trifon. A bad-tempered woman, I have to say, but as she spends all day asleep . . . So, shall it be Preference?'

We sat down to Preference for one-kopek stakes. Trifon won two and a half roubles off me and left late at night, very pleased with his winnings.

THE LOVERS' MEETING

ONE AUTUMN, AROUND mid-September, I was sitting in a birch wood. A fine drizzle had been falling since morning, now and then giving way to a spell of warm sunlight, for the weather was unsettled. Ragged white clouds would cover the sky, only to disperse for a moment, letting the bright, gentle azure peep through like a lovely eye. I sat and looked around me, and listened. The leaves rustled faintly overhead—their very sound told you what time of year it was. This was not the cheerful, fluttering laughter of spring, nor the soft whispering and leisurely chatter of summer, nor the timid, cold lisping of late autumn, but an almost inaudible, dreamlike murmur. A faint breeze was just touching the treetops. The depths of the wood, wet with rain, were constantly changing, as the sun now shone out, now hid behind clouds. Sometimes the whole wood became radiant, as if everything within it were smiling: the slender trunks of the sparse birch trees suddenly took on a gentle sheen like white silk, the little leaves covering the ground became burning specks of purest gold, and the handsome fronds of tall curly-headed ferns, already decked out in their autumn tints like overripe grapes, seemed to criss-cross and tangle together before my eyes. And the next moment everything around me turned faintly blue again, the bright colours were quenched in an instant, the birches lost their sheen and turned stark white, like fresh snow still untouched by the cold glint of a winter sun; and a sly, secret rustle of fine raindrops spread whispering through the trees. Almost all the leaves on the birches were still green, though markedly paler than before. Only a few young trees stood out, here and there, that were red or gold all over; and what a sight it was to see them burst into bright colour the instant the sun's rays broke through to touch them, bathing them in a patchwork of light, wherever it could penetrate the dense meshwork of thin branches overhead, washed clean by the glittering rain. Not a single bird could be heard—they had all fallen silent and gone into hiding, save for the rare ringing sound of the tomtit's mocking call, like a little steel bell. Before stopping in this birch wood, I had walked with my dog through a copse of tall aspens. I must confess that I'm not too fond of this tree, with its pale lilac trunk and grey-green metallic leaves, which it

raises as high as it can reach and fans out to tremble up
in the air. I dislike the ceaseless quivering of its untidy
round leaves that hang so awkwardly off their long
stems. Only on occasional summer evenings does it
look attractive, as it stands tall and solitary amidst low
bushes, and captures the reddening rays of the setting
sun, and trembles and glows, drenched from roots to
crown in an even, crimson-gold radiance. Or on a
clear, windy day, when it ripples and rustles noisily
against a blue sky, every leaf is caught up in the flow
and seems desperate to break away, fly off and soar into
the distance. But generally I'm not fond of that tree, so
I didn't stop to rest in the aspen thicket, but walked on
to the birch wood, nestled down under a little tree with
low-growing branches which would protect me from
the rain. Here I sat admiring the prospect around me
until I fell into that sweet, untroubled sleep which only
a hunter knows.

I can't say how long I slept, but when I opened my
eyes, the very depths of the wood were bathed in
sunlight, while all around me a bright blue sky shone—
almost sparkled—through the joyously rustling leaves.
The clouds had disappeared, scattered by the wind
that had sprung up; the weather had cleared, and you
could feel that peculiar dry freshness in the air which
fills your heart with exhilaration and almost always

promises a fine, clear evening after a rainy day. I was about to get up and try my luck again, when suddenly my eyes fell on a human figure sitting very still. I looked again. It was a young peasant girl, sitting twenty paces away from me, her head sunk in thought, both hands resting in her lap. One of her hands, half open, held a neat posy of wild flowers, which rose and fell gently over her checked skirt with every breath. A clean white smock, buttoned at her throat and wrists, fell in soft, short folds about her figure; a necklace of big yellow beads, wound twice round her neck, hung over her bosom. She was very pretty indeed. Her rich fair hair, a lovely ash-blond, was parted into two carefully combed loops peeping out from under a narrow red headband stretched round her ivory-white forehead. Her face and cheeks were faintly tanned that shade of gold that one only sees on delicate skin. I could not see her eyes, which remained downcast; but I could clearly see her fine, high eyebrows and long lashes: they were wet, and on one of her cheeks the sunlight picked out the trace of a dried tear that had run down to her rather pale lips. Her whole face was charming, and even her rather thick snub nose did not spoil it. I particularly liked her expression, so simple and meek, so sad, and so full of childlike wonder at her own sadness. She was evidently expecting someone. There was a faint crackle in the woods, and at once she raised her head and looked around. Through the transparent shadows I caught a fleeting glimpse of her eyes, large, clear and timid as a doe's. She listened for a few moments, staring wide-eyed towards the place where she had heard the faint sound; then she sighed, slowly turned away, bent forward even lower, and began slowly sorting her flowers. Her eyelids reddened, her lips twisted bitterly, and another tear rolled out from under her thick lashes, to rest bright and shining on her cheek. A long time passed. The poor girl did not move, save for a despairing gesture of her hands now and then; but she listened, listened . . . Once again there was a sound in the forest, and she gave a start. The sound did not stop, but drew nearer, becoming more distinct, till at last one could hear quick, resolute footsteps approaching. She straightened up nervously, her watchful face alight with tremulous expectation. Through the thicket there appeared the figure of a man walking fast. She looked, and suddenly flushed, then broke into a happy, joyous smile. She half rose to her feet, only to sink back, pale and confused, and at last raised her tremulous, almost pleading eyes to the man who had stopped by her side.

I looked curiously at him from my hiding place. I have to say that he did not make a good impression.

Everything pointed to his being the pampered valet of a rich young gentleman. His clothing betrayed some pretension to style and dandified nonchalance: he was wearing a short bronze-coloured coat, probably passed on from his master, buttoned up to the neck, a pink cravat with lilac ends, and a black velvet cap decorated with gold braid, pulled right down to his eyebrows. The round collar of his white shirt dug mercilessly into his ears and cut into his cheeks; his starched cuffs hid the whole of his hands down to the crooked red fingers adorned with gold and silver rings, one decorated with turquoise forget-me-nots. He had a fresh, red, insolent face—the kind which, in my experience, almost always annoys men but, sadly, very often appeals to women. He was evidently doing his best to give his coarse features an air of bored contempt; he kept screwing up his milky-grey eyes (tiny enough without that), scowling, letting his mouth droop, yawning affectedly, or, with careless but rather clumsy nonchalance, adjusting the dashing curls over his temples and fingering the yellow hairs that sprouted on his thick upper lip. In short, he gave himself insufferable airs. He had started putting on this act as soon as he caught sight of the young peasant girl waiting for him. He sauntered casually up to her, stopped and shrugged his shoulders, thrust both hands into his coat pockets, and scarcely sparing the poor girl a cursory, indifferent glance, lowered himself to the ground.

'So,' he began, still looking away to one side, swinging his leg and yawning, 'been here long?'

The girl couldn't reply straight away.

'Yes, Viktor Alexandrich,' she whispered at last, almost inaudibly. 'A long time.'

'Oh.'—He took off his cap and swept his hand majestically over his thick, stiffly curled hair, which grew almost down to his eyebrows. 'Well, I almost forgot. And besides, this rain!' (He yawned once more.) 'I've got lots to do—can't see to everything, and he keeps yelling at me. We're leaving tomorrow . . .'

'Tomorrow?' the girl exclaimed with a startled look.

'Yes, tomorrow . . . Oh, come on, come on, please,' he added quickly and crossly, seeing her trembling all over and quietly drooping her head. 'Akulina, please, stop crying. You know I hate that.' (And he wrinkled his snub nose.) 'Or I'll go away right now . . . How stupid—blubbering like that!'

'No, I won't, I won't,' said Akulina hurriedly, making an effort to swallow her tears. 'So you're leaving tomorrow?' she added after a pause. 'And when will God grant that we see each other again, Viktor Alexandrich?'

'Oh, we will, we will. If not next year, then later on. My master wants to go to Petersburg and enter the service, I believe,' he went on, giving his words a care-less nasal twang. 'And we might go abroad too.'

'You'll forget me, Viktor Alexandrich,' she said sadly.

'No, why should I? I shan't forget you. But you've got to be a sensible girl, don't act silly, do as your father says . . . But I shan't forget you—no-o-o.' (And he stretched himself coolly and yawned again.)

'Don't forget me, Viktor Alexandrich,' she went on imploringly. 'It seems to me . . . I've loved you so, so much . . . I've done everything for you . . . You're telling me to do as my father says, Viktor Alexandrich . . . but how can I?'

'Why not?' (He seemed to be speaking from his stomach, as he lay on his back with his hands under his head.)

'What do you mean, Viktor Alexandrich? You know perfectly well why not . . .' She stopped. Viktor fingered his steel watch chain.

'Akulina, you're not a stupid girl,' he said at last. 'So don't you talk rubbish. This is for your own good, can't you understand? Of course you're not stupid, you're not just a peasant, I mean; and your mother wasn't always a peasant either. But still you've got no education, so of course you've got to do what people tell you.'

'But it's scary, Viktor Alexandrich.'

'O-oh, what nonsense, my good girl! What is there to be scared of?—What have you got there?' he added, moving closer to her. 'Flowers?'

'Yes,' Akulina answered miserably. 'This is some wild tansy I picked,' she went on, brightening up a bit, 'it does the little calves good. And these here are marigolds, for the scrofula. Just look, what a pretty flower it is, I've never seen such a lovely one in my life. And these are forget-me-nots, and those are sweet violets . . . And I picked these for you,' she added, reaching under the yellow tansy to bring out a little posy of blue cornflowers, tied up with a thin blade of grass. 'Would you like them?'

Viktor stretched out a languid hand to take them, sniffed them carelessly and began twisting them in his fingers, raising his eyes with an expression of pensive self-importance. Akulina gazed at him. Her sorrowful eyes were filled with tender devotion, humble adoration and love. She was afraid of him, and dared not weep, and was bidding him farewell, and admiring him for the last time; while he lay sprawled like a sultan, accepting her adoration with magnanimous tolerance and condescension. I must admit that I felt indignant as I looked at his red face, whose mask of contemptuous indifference could not hide a satisfied and surfeited vanity. Akulina was so lovely at that moment; her very soul lay open before him, trusting and passionate, full of longing and tender affection, while he . . . dropping her cornflowers into the grass, he took a round eyeglass with a bronze rim out of his coat pocket and started screwing it into his eye. But however hard he tried to keep it in place by frowning, pulling up his cheek and even using his nose, the glass kept falling out into his hand.

'What's that?' Akulina eventually asked him in astonishment.

'A lorgnette.'

'What's it for?'

'To see better.'

'Can I have a look?'

Viktor scowled, but handed her the glass.

'Mind you don't break it!'

'I shan't break it, don't worry.' Timidly she raised the glass to her eye. 'I can't see a thing,' she said innocently.

'Go on, screw up your eye, then,' he retorted in the tones of a disgruntled instructor. She screwed up the eye that was looking through the glass.

'Not that one, that's the wrong one, you idiot! The other one!' exclaimed Viktor, and without letting her put right her mistake, he took back the lorgnette.

Akulina blushed, laughed faintly, and turned away.

'No good for our sort, I suppose,' she said.

'I should think not!'

The poor girl said nothing, but gave a deep sigh.

'Oh, Viktor Alexandrich, what are we going to do without you!' she suddenly exclaimed.

Viktor wiped the lorgnette on his coat-tail and put it back in his pocket.

'Yes, yes,' he said after a pause. 'It'll be hard for you to begin with, of course.' He patted her condescendingly on the shoulder. She gently removed his hand from her shoulder and kissed it timidly. 'Well, yes, indeed, you really are a nice girl,' he went on with a complacent smile, 'but what's to be done! You can see for yourself—the master and I can't stay here, can we? Soon it'll be winter, and winter in the country, you know yourself—it's just disgusting. Petersburg is nothing like that! They have such wonders there—a silly girl like you could never imagine them in your dreams. Such houses, such streets, and the cultured society they have—unbelievable!'

Akulina was listening to every word, completely engrossed, with her mouth slightly open, like a child.

'Anyway,' he added, rolling over on the grass, 'why am I telling you all this? You can't understand a word of it.'

'Why not, Viktor Alexandrich? I can understand, I understood everything.'

'Oh yes, just look at you!'

Akulina hung her head.

'You never used to talk to me like that before, Viktor Alexandrich,' she said, without looking up.

'Before? . . . Before! Get along with you! . . . Before!' he said, putting on an indignant air.

Both sat silent for a little.

'Anyway, I've got to go,' said Viktor, already raising himself on one elbow.

'Wait a bit longer!' Akulina implored him.

'What's the point? . . . I've already said goodbye to you.'

'Wait a bit!' Akulina said again.

Viktor lay back down and started whistling. Akulina never took her eyes off him. I could see that she was close to breaking down—her lips twitched, her pale cheeks became a little flushed . . .

'Viktor Alexandrich,' she eventually said in a broken voice, 'it's not right of you, it's not right, Viktor Alexandrich, really it isn't!'

'What's not right?' he demanded with a scowl, raising his head to look at her.

'It isn't right, Viktor Alexandrich. You might at least say something kind to me now we're parting, just a word, to a poor lonely little thing like me . . .'

'What am I supposed to say to you, then?'

'I don't know. You know better than me, Viktor Alexandrich. Here you are, going away, and not a word for me . . . What have I done to deserve that?'

'What an odd girl you are! What can I do about it?'

'One little word from you—'

'Just listen to you, going on and on about the same thing,' he said irritably, and stood up.

'Don't be cross with me, Viktor Alexandrich,' she said hastily, barely holding back her tears.

'I'm not cross, but you're being stupid . . . What do you want? You know I can't marry you! I can't, can I? So what is it you want? What is it?'

He thrust his face forward as if waiting for an answer, and spread out his hands.

'I don't . . . I don't want anything,' she stammered, hardly daring to hold out her trembling hands to him. 'But just a little word from you, to say goodbye . . .'

And her tears poured down her face.

'Well, off you go, crying again,' said Viktor coolly, putting a hand behind his head to tilt his cap over his brow.

'I don't want anything,' she repeated between sobs, hiding her face in her hands. 'But what's it going to be like for me with my family now, how can I stand it? What's going to happen to me, what'll become of me, poor thing? They'll marry me off to someone hateful, poor little me . . . Oh, poor me!'

'Sing away, sing away,' muttered Viktor under his breath, shuffling his feet where he stood.

'Couldn't he have said just one word to me, just one? . . . Just to say, Akulina, I . . .'

She couldn't go on. All at once she broke down in heart-rending sobs, fell face down on the grass, and wept bitterly. Her whole body was racked, her neck jerked backwards . . . The grief she had held back for so long now flooded out. Viktor stood over her a while, waited, then shrugged his shoulders, turned on his heel and strode briskly away.

A few moments passed . . . She quietened down, raised her head, jumped to her feet, looked about her and flung up her arms. She tried to run after him, but her legs gave way and she fell to her knees . . . I couldn't bear to watch, and hurried towards her. But the instant she became aware of me—who knows where she found the strength—she uttered a faint shriek, jumped to her feet and vanished through the trees, leaving her flowers scattered on the ground.

I was left standing there. I picked up the posy of cornflowers and walked out of the thicket into the field. The sun had sunk low in the clear, pale sky; its rays too seemed to have grown pale and cold. They were not shining, but diffusing an even, almost watery light. There was just half an hour left till sunset, but there was no evening glow in the sky. A gusty wind raced towards me over the dry yellow stubble, blowing little crumpled leaves up into the air and sweeping them past me, over the path and along the edge of the wood. The whole side of the wood that faced the field like a wall was trembling and glittering with tiny gleams, sharp but not bright; and over the reddish leaves on the ground, and the blades of grass, and the sticks of straw, there glistened innumerable strands of autumn spiders' webs, trembling in the wind. I halted . . .

I felt sad. Through the fresh but cheerless smile of fading nature, I could sense a dismal apprehension as the impending winter stealthily approached. High above me a cautious raven flew by, its wings sharply and heavily cleaving the air; turning its head, it gave me a sideways look, soared up and disappeared behind the woods with a sharp caw. A big flock of pigeons flew merrily up from a threshing floor, suddenly whirled about in a column and scattered busily over the fields— a sure sign of autumn. Someone was clattering along in an empty cart behind the bare hilltop nearby . . .

I went back home. But the image of poor Akulina remained with me a long time; and I still have her cornflowers, faded long ago . . .

PUSHKIN PRESS

Pushkin Press was founded in 1997, and publishes novels, essays, memoirs, children's books—everything from timeless classics to the urgent and contemporary.

This book is part of the Pushkin Collection of paperbacks, designed to be as satisfying as possible to hold and to enjoy. It is typeset in Monotype Baskerville, based on the transitional English serif typeface designed in the mid-eighteenth century by John Baskerville. It was litho-printed on Munken Premium White Paper and notch-bound by the independently owned printer TJ International in Padstow, Cornwall. The cover, with French flaps, was printed on Rives Linear Bright White paper. The paper and cover board are both acid-free and Forest Stewardship Council (FSC) certified.

Pushkin Press publishes the best writing from around the world—great stories, beautifully produced, to be read and read again.

STEFAN ZWEIG · EDGAR ALLAN POE · ISAAC BABEL
TOMÁS GONZÁLEZ · ULRICH PLENZDORF · JOSEPH KESSEL
VELIBOR ČOLIĆ · LOUISE DE VILMORIN · MARCEL AYMÉ
ALEXANDER PUSHKIN · MAXIM BILLER · JULIEN GRACQ
BROTHERS GRIMM · HUGO VON HOFMANNSTHAL
GEORGE SAND · PHILIPPE BEAUSSANT · IVÁN REPILA
E.T.A. HOFFMANN · ALEXANDER LERNET-HOLENIA
YASUSHI INOUE · HENRY JAMES · FRIEDRICH TORBERG
ARTHUR SCHNITZLER · ANTOINE DE SAINT-EXUPÉRY
MACHI TAWARA · GAITO GAZDANOV · HERMANN HESSE
LOUIS COUPERUS · JAN JACOB SLAUERHOFF
PAUL MORAND · MARK TWAIN · PAUL FOURNEL
ANTAL SZERB · JONA OBERSKI · MEDARDO FRAILE
HÉCTOR ABAD · PETER HANDKE · ERNST WEISS
PENELOPE DELTA · RAYMOND RADIGUET · PETR KRÁL
ITALO SVEVO · RÉGIS DEBRAY · BRUNO SCHULZ · TEFFI
EGON HOSTOVSKÝ · JOHANNES URZIDIL · JÓZEF WITTLIN